ROSE GARDENER'S FLORIST

THE PROVIDENCE STREET SHOPS
BOOK TWO

BONNIE DEE

DRAGONBLADE PUBLISHING, INC.

Text by Bonnie Dee
Cover by Dar Albert

Dragonblade Publishing, Inc. is an imprint of Kathryn Le Veque Novels, Inc.
P.O. Box 7968
La Verne CA 91750
ceo@dragonbladepublishing.com

Produced in the United States of America

First Edition January 2021
Print Edition

ARE YOU SIGNED UP FOR DRAGONBLADE'S BLOG?

You'll get the latest news and information on exclusive giveaways, exclusive excerpts, coming releases, sales, free books, cover reveals and more.

Check out our complete list of authors, too!

No spam, no junk. That's a promise!

Sign Up Here

www.dragonbladepublishing.com

Dearest Reader;

Thank you for your support of a small press. At Dragonblade Publishing, we strive to bring you the highest quality Historical Romance from the some of the best authors in the business. Without your support, there is no 'us', so we sincerely hope you adore these stories and find some new favorite authors along the way.

Happy Reading!

CEO, Dragonblade Publishing

ADDITIONAL DRAGONBLADE BOOKS BY AUTHOR BONNIE DEE

The Providence Street Shops Series

Hattie Glover's Millinery

Rose Gardener's Florist

CHAPTER ONE

London 1907

ROSE GARDENER'S FLORIST. Rose admired the sign above her brand-new shop for the hundredth time; gold letters against a green background with the stem of a red rose twined around the "R." She had considered adding a smaller line below: *Better Bouquets for a Brighter World*, but her friend Hattie had convinced her it was too much verbiage and the customer's eye could not take in so many words.

"Simple and eye-catching is always best," the milliner had said.

The new word *verbiage* was to be added to Rose's *lexicon*, another term she had learned from Hattie Glover while working as her assistant. If one wanted to elevate oneself in the world, one must speak properly, even using proper diction in one's thoughts. Rose continually worked to eradicate all traces of her former accent, except when she visited home, where her family would sneer at her for putting on airs.

Although it was still early in the morning, heat filled the air with muggy moisture. Perhaps this would be the last hot spell before summer ebbed into fall. The rainbow array of summer flowers would shift to golds and oranges. Rose might insert cattails, wheat stalks or autumn leaves into her bouquets. There was no one to tell her such common things didn't belong in a proper floral arrangement. How wonderful to have the freedom to design as *unconventionally* as she wished. Living her dream of owning a florist had Rose's arm fairly bruised from pinching to see if she would awaken.

With a last look up Providence Street at the row of neat storefronts with colorful awnings, Rose went inside to check on the merchandise she'd purchased from the market earlier that morning. One must be at Covent Garden before dawn to meet the growers of fresh flowers, fruits and vegetables brought in from the country. But Rose didn't mind rising far earlier than the sun. It reminded her of when she was small and would go with Gram to sort through the floral remains on the cobblestones. She and Gram would then spend the day selling nosegays to the toffs. Much had changed since then, yet a part of her would always be that skinny, knobby-kneed girl wearing a too-large, patched dress.

Rose banished memories and focused on pulling dead leaves and flower heads. She gave the flowers a spray of water to keep them fresh. The multi-colored blooms in buckets were set on risers of varying levels to create a wall of color on one side of the shop.

From the back room, she brought up an arrangement for the display window. The bouquet was so wide and tall, she could not see over the flowers. The loaded urn grew heavier with each step as she staggered blindly toward the front window.

"Let me help you with that!"

Rose yipped in surprise. The door was propped open to catch any stray breeze, so the bell had not announced a customer's arrival. Unseen hands touched hers in an attempt to relieve her of the urn. Rose did not let go, and for a moment, she and her invisible helper played tug-o-war over possession of the flowers.

They both released their grip at the same time. The urn slipped from her grasp.

"No!" Rose had spent nearly an hour and used many expensive flowers to create the elaborate bouquet intended to catch the eye of passers-by. It was a sales tool she could not afford to lose.

The customer grappled with the urn, caught it, staggered backward, and ended up on his knees with the arrangement clutched to his chest. Through the greenery, hazel eyes peered at Rose through round spectacles. "Sorry! I was trying to help."

"And a capital job you did of it, old boy," a familiar voice drew Rose's attention from her would-be rescuer to Guy Hardy, her investor and friend.

Guy relieved the sandy-haired man of his burden of flowers. When the fellow rose, he unfolded like a long-legged bird to tower nearly a head above Guy, who was not a short man by any means. The stork helped Guy place the arrangement in the window with the best blooms facing the street.

"Whew!" Guy exclaimed. "You'll give yourself a bad back, Copper Top. I recommend smaller and lighter bouquets."

"Large ornate ones draw the eye, and please, stop calling me Copper Top," Rose chided Hardy, who had become more like a brother to her than either of her own. Neither Dale nor Danny had helped make improvements on the storefront she rented, although to be fair, they worked all day and Dale had a family to look after. Meanwhile, Guy had been here almost every day, painting, building and performing other tasks she could not afford to hire out. Part of his reason for dedicating so much labor had been to distract himself from his heartache over losing Hattie. Still, Rose had still appreciated the help.

Guy patted her head then drew his hand away as if burned. "Maybe Fire Top would be better. It is so very red."

Rose clicked her tongue in feigned annoyance. Her gaze turned to the tall stranger, clearly a friend of Guy's.

Guy clapped him on the back, driving him a step closer to Rose. "Miss Rose Gardener, may I introduce you to my friend, Mr. William Carmody, whom you may have heard me mention before."

Rose nodded. "My chum Will" had featured in a number of Guy's stories. They partnered in tennis, fencing and other club activities reserved for rich men. But this fellow was not the man Rose had pictured. For an athlete, Mr. Carmody seemed incredibly awkward. His broad shoulders hunched—a tall man's attempt to appear shorter—and he did not quite meet her gaze as they were introduced.

"Pleased to meet you, Miss Gardener." Carmody pushed his glasses up his nose with one finger.

Rose smiled at him. "Thank you for trying to help me."

"'Trying' being the operative word," Guy joked.

"I'm sorry I nearly dropped your flowers. Clumsy of me." The man's low-pitched voice seemed cool somehow, like a smooth stream flowing by without a ripple. Rose wanted to dip her hand in the water and ruffle its surface.

"How do you do, Mr. Carmody. I'm pleased to make your acquaintance." She used careful diction as she held out her hand.

He stared at it for a moment as if deciding whether to shake hands with a mere shop girl. Had she made a social error? Rose's smile evaporated, but before she could withdraw, his large hand engulfed hers in a single pump before letting go.

"Your store is very nice. I admire your, um"—he gestured toward the buckets—"flowers."

"Thank you," she replied. Mr. Carmody's stiff manner put her off, even if he *had* tried to help her carry the urn. Guy's friend or no, it seemed Carmody was snobbish and superior with his formality and refusal to look at her.

Rose turned her attention to Guy. "Will you be stopping by the millinery next, or have you already been?"

Since Guy and Hattie's happy reunion several months ago, they rarely spent a day apart. He was always either coming or going from the milliner's shop.

"I thought I'd bring my fiancée a bouquet to brighten her day, before Carmody and I engage in a fencing match. Peonies, please. Such a delightful scent."

"They are not in season. But she should like these pink roses."

Rose went to select the blooms for her friend's bouquet. As she passed Mr. Carmody, he moved out of her way, bumping his elbow into a metal stand holding cards for funeral wreaths: *At rest with Our Savior, Long Loved—Too Soon Lost,* and so on. He caught the display before it could topple and steadied it.

"Sorry. I'm so sorry." He knelt to gather the heartfelt pronouncements from the floor and place them back into the rack.

"Don't worry, Mr. Carmody. I will take care of those later." Rose would have liked to suggest he leave the shop before he created a more serious disaster, but this was Guy's dearest friend, so she remained polite.

"Listen, Red..." Guy ignored Carmody as if he were used to his friend's clumsiness. "Can you make a bouquet that proclaims *Please set a date?* It has been some time since I presented Hattie with a ring. I'm ready for newly-wed bliss, but my dearest is ever cautious, as you well know."

"That's a lot to ask of a bouquet. I would not apply too much pressure. When Hattie has considered the matter from every angle she will be ready. Wasn't I right when I told you to wait for her forgiveness?"

"Yes, my wise counselor, you did."

"Then don't rush her about this once-in-a-lifetime decision." Rose said, as she wrapped the plump pink roses in paper and handed the bouquet to Guy.

He sighed dramatically. "I will rein in my impatience and hold my tongue. I just needed you to tell me so."

Rose glanced at the giant who had withdrawn to a corner, one hand crossed over the other in front of him as if to keep them from flailing about. Guy was apparently not shy about expressing his emotions in front of his friend. If he deemed Will Carmody trustworthy and loyal, perhaps the man was not so bad.

Rose offered Carmody another smile.

He grimaced and looked away. What a snob!

Just then, the first actual customer of the day entered the shop, so Guy bid Rose farewell.

Mr. Carmody did, too. "Good morning. That is, good day, Miss Gardener. Nice to have met. It was your pleasure…that is, a pleasure to have met. You. Today."

He ducked his head to avoid the lintel as he passed through the doorway.

Rose shook her head and rolled her eyes.

After that, she had no time, or reason, to think of the odd man until much later when she picked up one of the funeral notes from the floor: *Gone but Not Forgotten.*

She thought of Carmody's height and looming presence—somewhat as she had envisioned Frankenstein's monster in Mrs. Shelley's thrilling book, though not stitched together from body parts. And the monster would not have worn a scholarly pair of spectacles perched upon his nose. The thought of Carmody's large hands seizing her body to carry her away made her shiver. Oddly enough, it wasn't fear, but another sort of inexplicable excitement that zipped through her with the speed of lightning.

What was it about Mr. Carmody that haunted her long after his rangy frame no longer filled her doorway? He might be ungainly, but there was a strange magnetism about his presence that made him difficult to forget. If Guy Hardy was pure energy filling any room he entered and drawing all attention, William Carmody was his dark counterpart, the shadow to his light.

Too bad Carmody was also stuck up. Under other circumstances, Rose might have been interested in knowing him better. After all, he was her investor's best mate.

IDIOT! FOOL! CLUMSY buffoon! No wonder pretty Miss Rose had laughed at him standing in the corner like a troll. She was probably laughing still at his clownish ways. And the stammering! He had hardly been able to put two intelligible words together.

"Are you suffering heatstroke, Carmody?" Guy asked. "Perhaps you should go home and lie down with a damp cloth on your head rather than engage in a strenuous fencing match which you know I will ultimately win."

Will closed his fingers together. "Shut it."

Guy laughed as he led the way to Hattie Glover's Millinery several doors down from the florist. Will would be equally uncomfortable in a room full of ladies' hats and sundries, but at least there was no Miss Gardener to make him act like an utter fool.

"Good morning, William," Hattie greeted him, when he entered.

"Good morning, Miss Glover." Will remained near the door this time so he would not knock over a mannequin head.

Hardy offered his fiancée the roses. "Good morning, my dearest."

She buried her nose in a bloom and inhaled deeply. "They are beautiful."

"The petals are not as soft as your lips." Guy leaned over the display counter to murmur something that earned an even bigger smile.

How at ease the fellow was with women. All women. Not only his beloved, but the entire gender. Will had never been able to speak easily with females, except for Penny. He wasn't certain how he'd become shy. In the luck of the draw, his elder brother Rupert and younger sister Penelope had inherited charisma and confidence, while Will ended up with insecurity and self-doubt.

He was only truly good at one thing—study, and he'd made it his life's work to learn all he could about every subject under the sun. With his extensive library and prodigious memory, this made for a lot of information crammed into his brain. But to what purpose? What did it matter if he knew everything in the world? That was a mystery he had yet to solve.

Guy bid farewell to his fiancée at last. "I will see you later, my love."

"If you're lucky," Hattie retorted. Then she smiled at Will. "You must join us for supper soon."

"I would welcome the invitation. Thank you, Mrs. Glover."

"Please, call me Hattie. We are too dear of friends for such formality."

Will followed Guy from the foreign sanctum of women's hats and sundries to the bright outdoors. Immediately he began to sweat under layers of clothes. "The day is already hot and it is not yet noon. Are you certain you wish to exercise this morning? Perhaps a quiet game of billiards instead…"

"Have to get you moving, or you'll rot away indoors." Guy briskly strode down the sidewalk.

"Might I point out that the fencing is also indoors?" But Will amiably fell into step beside his friend.

SOON THEY WERE at the club, suited, masked, and thrusting foils at one another. They lunged and parried around the piste in a sportsman's minuet.

Will was not as fit as Guy, but managed quite well when his strategic foresight met Guy's erratic actions. As in chess, Will could calculate moves ahead, particularly knowing his friend's style as well as he did. Ultimately, he scored the most points, vanquishing his opponent without need for a lethal blow.

Will pushed off the épée mask and ran a hand through his matted hair, blowing a breath upward to cool his face. He reached for his spectacles to wipe steam from the lenses.

Guy joined him at the side of the mat. "Half-blind and you still bested me. How is it you are so agile in a match."

"Yet so clumsy the rest of the time?" Will completed his thought.

"I cannot answer that. All I know is that I made a fool of myself today at the florist's shop."

"Nonsense. Very gallant of you to help Rose. I didn't think to do so, just watched her struggle with the urn. As for knocking over the display, it was in the way. Anyone might have done so."

"But my parting words were abysmal. Why do I grow so tongue-tied I can scarcely speak when confronted by a pretty woman—or any woman?"

"Lack of practice." Guy gave Will a curious look. "You find Rose pretty? I suppose she is, but I hardly see it. She is like a sister." He shed the top of his uniform, fanned himself and stated bluntly, "You fancy her."

"I don't even know the woman."

"Yet you have visions of bright red hair and a saucy upturned nose dancing through your mind. Admit it."

"That is not true." Will turned away, heading toward the changing rooms.

Guy followed after. "I don't know quite how I feel about that. If you were to woo her and things don't go well, it would be awkward for me. My best friend and my business partner, not to mention Hattie's friend. Decidedly awkward."

"Good of you to immediately expect the worst outcome and how it might affect you." Will rushed to add, "Not that I would attempt to woo the lady, who is far too young for an old bachelor like me."

"Rose is twenty-two."

"And I am thirty. Nearly a full decade's difference. Besides which, she is bright and lively, and I am as dull as a post. A woman like her could have no interest in me whatsoever."

"You've given this matter a great deal of thought for someone who isn't interested."

Will fell silent. Refusing to engage was the only hope of turning Guy away from a subject once he'd seized hold of it. But his friend remained doggedly determined.

"Hattie and I might invite you both to supper, giving our best friends the opportunity to become better acquainted. What could be more natural? That would give you a chance to press your cause."

"Do *not* do that, I beg of you. I cannot think of a more excruciating way to spend an evening."

Guy managed to drop the subject until they were both cleaned up, dressed, and on the street once more.

"I understand you wish to woo Rose at your own pace. But, my friend, that is often at the speed of a glacier melting. Might I make a recommendation to get you started? The woman sells flowers. You have a mother, a sister, and many aunts and female cousins. Purchase a bouquet—often. Become her best customer. When the timing is right by your prehistoric timepiece, ask her on an outing."

"Hardy."

"Yes, Will?"

"Do not insinuate yourself into my romantic life. I am quite content to go on exactly as I am."

"But you could be even happier with a blue-eyed redhead, who possesses a sweet disposition seasoned with a little pepper." Guy brandished an invisible foil. "Point."

CHAPTER TWO

AFTER A BUSY day of helping customers and snatching time in between to fill orders, Rose was nearly too exhausted to move, let alone attend a meeting. But she had pledged herself to the Women's Social and Political Union, which met this evening. A woman's right to vote was a cause she believed in deeply. If she gave up simply because it was an inconvenience, what sort of suffragette was she?

In some ways life had been easier as an assistant at the millinery. After work, her evenings had been her own without the constant worry over the shop's success. Running a store, she now appreciated Hattie's burden of ownership as never before.

Another big change was the utter quiet of living alone. As Rose prepared a solitary meal in her flat above the shop, she almost missed the chatter of the girls at Miss Cecily's boarding house. Her friends there had shared stories about themselves or their workdays at a shop or office. Before that, Rose had lived in a raucous family of six in a two-room, cold-water flat. She'd longed for peace all her life. Now she'd gotten it and the silence was sometimes deafening.

But she oughtn't to foolishly bemoan things she had lost rather than celebrating everything she had gained. Rose shook off her momentary melancholy and prepared to go out.

The WSPU were assembling at a member's home, one with a drawing room large enough to accommodate many members. Rose found herself in a wealthy part of the city in a house she could not have imagined as a child in Spitalfields. The physical distance from that slum to Mayfair was no more than six miles, but it may as well have been from the earth to the moon. She often felt like an alien visitor to this lofty world.

What began for Rose as one-time attendance at an open rally had led to membership in this union of women. But the tone of the WSPU had changed after their proposed suffrage bill was voted down. Their demonstrations had become increasingly violent. Members, including Emmeline Pankhurst and her daughters, had been arrested following attacks on police, politicians and public buildings. Rose feared risking her fledgling business by affiliating herself with the WSPU's open aggression, but how could she inform Mrs. Pankhurst of that, when the leader had taken Rose under her wing?

Arriving late to the meeting, Rose slid into an empty chair as Christabel Pankhurst spoke of a planned demonstration. The young lady sitting beside Rose was not one she recognized. She was a heavyset, dark-haired girl with wide brown eyes riveted on the speaker. Rose became more interested in the newcomer's reaction than in the debate that followed.

As the meeting turned into fervent discussion of differing opinions, Rose addressed her seat mate. "Your first meeting? It is a bit overwhelming isn't it?"

The young lady nodded. "I'm not certain I belong here. Everyone seems so knowledgeable and committed to the cause."

"Have you come with a friend?" Rose could not imagine why the newcomer sat alone.

"Actually, I overheard mention of a secret suffrage meeting and invited myself."

She showed more spirit than Rose had expected. "Well, I'm glad you came. It is nice to sit beside someone who may feel even more out of place than I often do." She offered her hand. "I am Rose Gardener."

The woman shook it, but hesitated before revealing her name. "You may call me Violet."

"One of my favorite flowers! I am a florist." How proud she felt to say it. "Working women like me have only recently been invited to attend, as the WSPU has been limited to the upper class. I am glad of it, for it is only through solidarity of all women, high born and low, that we might accomplish our goal."

"Will having the vote matter when men possess all true power?" Violet's eyes glistened and she swallowed hard before continuing. "The vote would not be of any use in my situation. Nothing can change my fate."

Rose offered her handkerchief. "Shall we leave the meeting and have a private chat? I know I am a stranger to you, but we are all meant to be sisters here. We ought to share each other's trials."

Violet hastily dried her eyes and returned Hattie's handkerchief. "I must go. Thank you for your kindness, Miss Gardener."

Rose recalled the safe haven Hattie's shop had been to Miss Jennifer Pruett in her time of need. She would like to offer that same sort of sanctuary. "If you change your mind and desire a listening ear, you might find me at my shop on Providence Street."

The finely dressed young woman nodded, then rose and hurried from the room.

Rose was very tempted to go after her. The decision of where to hold a grand rally followed by a march on Parliament paled in comparison to the very real distress exhibited by the mysterious Violet. But someone was asking her about providing floral arrangements for the event, so Rose stayed and involved herself in the meeting.

SEVERAL DAYS LATER, Rose stood misting gladioluses and praying they would not wilt before she sold them. She fought an ongoing battle against an especially hot summer. No one wanted a limp bouquet. Her new agreement with a grower to deliver stock directly to her door saved her those early morning trips to Covent Garden. So far, quality flowers had arrived with satisfying punctuality. No customer uttered a negative word about their freshness, and she intended to keep it that way.

Rose stepped away from the wall of flowers and bumped into a different sort of wall, something hard, unyielding and human. She shrieked, whirled around and sprayed the silent intruder with her misting bottle.

The man retreated, brushing droplets of water from his face. "I apologize. I didn't intend to frighten you. I should have announced my presence, but I thought you heard me enter the store."

"No. I did not!" Rose snapped. Frankenstein's monster had returned. She gritted her teeth and tried to remember that all customers must be treated like honored guests. But honestly, why was the fellow looming right behind her?

She managed a weak smile. "May I help you, Mr. Carmody?"

He had removed his spectacles and now wiped the glass in nervous circles with his handkerchief. "Yes. I, um, need to buy… that is, my aunt is ill and having a birthday so I must buy her a bouquet."

"How kind of you. Do you know what sort of flowers your aunt prefers? I have some lovely gladioluses today."

Carmody's gaze darted around the shop as if seeking an exit. "Red," he blurted. "She likes red."

"I'm afraid I have no red gladioluses. How about red roses? Or perhaps a potted gardenia which will last longer?"

"Roses, I think. Yes. Roses." He cleared his throat and added, "Fragrant and pretty like, um, you." His face turned as scarlet as the flowers and he stared at his feet. "My weak attempt at charm. Hardy has a knack for it, but I am hopeless. Please pretend I did not say that."

This fellow truly was the opposite of his friend in every way. Still, his clumsy attempt to compliment her was rather adorable.

Rose abruptly understood that Carmody had not been too arrogant to speak to her on their first meeting. He was simply tongue-tied with shyness. A warm wave of sympathy at his distress swept through her, demanding she put him at ease.

"All is well, Mr. Carmody. I accept your kind praise in the spirit it was given. Now, may I show you the roses and make up a bouquet?"

He nodded and moved his large body with great care around the shop, keeping his elbows to himself as he passed the bereavement display. *Rest In His Love Forever.*

When she showed him the array of blooms from purest white, to yellow and pink, to deepest ruby, Carmody bowed over the roses and inhaled deeply. His eyelids closed. The thickness of the spectacles enhanced the long lashes fanning across his cheeks. Rose felt a little hitch in her chest at the sight of his pleasure, as if she were witnessing a private moment.

He straightened, regaining his height. "*Rosa ruber*, a woody perennial of the genus *Rosa*, in the family *Rosacae*, is it not?"

"I, uh, suppose so," she responded to his scientific identification. "I just sell them. I do not know Latin names. Only that they smell nice." Apparently, his awkwardness was catching.

She selected the best flowers, stems dripping wet from the bucket. "How many?"

"Two dozen." His voice grew so quiet she could scarcely hear.

"That many? They are quite expensive."

He waved a hand as if shooing away a fly. "No matter. She is my favorite niece, um, aunt."

His slip told her there was no sick relative celebrating a birthday. That meant something else had brought him to the shop, and there was only one likely reason. Rose cringed as she realized he'd invented a pretext to see her, a flattering but frightening thought. She was not interested in Mr. Carmody, but didn't want to offend him by rejecting him. This wasn't some would-be lothario flirting with her, but Guy's dearest friend, which put her in an awkward position.

Her nervous tension distracted her from attending to the roses. A sharp point bit into her palm and left behind not a light scratch but a jagged tear. She yelped, tried to avoid dropping the flowers and succeeded in grabbing a fistful of thorns.

Mr. Carmody wrested the roses from her grip with one hand and took a handkerchief from his pocket with the other. "Bind your hand until I can tend to it," he ordered in an authoritative tone.

Rose mutely did as he bid.

He set the flowers aside and escorted her to the work room as if he had been there before. Locating the sink, he held her bleeding hand while pumping water over it. "Have you any salve or bandages?"

With his thumb pressing tight against her palm to slow the bleeding, she couldn't think straight. "I have… I'm afraid I don't. I haven't needed any before."

He pushed his glasses into place and leaned to examine her wound. "I think I see a bit of thorn embedded. Do you have tweezers with which I might pluck it out?"

She shook her head. "I suppose I am ill-prepared for accidents."

"I will attempt to capture it with my nails with your permission." His courtly manner made her smile.

"Please do."

He peered more closely at her wound, warm breath grazing her skin as he painstakingly teased out the sharp point that had broken off.

"Steady on. Nearly there," he soothed, when Rose whimpered.

But it was not pain that prompted the sound. His nearness and kindness stirred something inside her which rose to the surface as a little moan.

"Aha! I've got you." Carmody plucked a dark bit from her throbbing palm and flicked it into the sink. "Now for a disinfectant. Have you any alcohol or perhaps a bottle of vinegar?"

"Yes, I do, for shining the windows." She pointed out a bottle under the sink.

When her rescuer doused her wound with the astringent, she moaned again.

He regarded her with luminescent eyes enlarged by the spectacle lenses. "I am sorry to hurt you, Miss Gardener, but it is necessary to stave off infection."

"Of course. Thank you for your aid, Mr. Carmody. I appreciate it."

More than he could have known, for at no time in her memory had anyone treated her with such tender care. The Gardener family was not prone to warmth or gentleness.

Her knight bound her hand in his kerchief again, tying the makeshift bandage tightly. "Be certain to treat your hand again later today and put on a fresh cloth, won't you? If any redness or swelling occurs, go to a physician at once."

Rose nodded, astounded by the man's shift from shyness to authority. She touched the fine linen stained with her blood. "How do you know so much about doctoring?"

"Through my reading. One never knows what topics might prove useful, so I learn as much as I can about many things."

"Well, this was certainly useful knowledge to have. I can't thank you enough. Now, let me make up that bouquet—for your aunt."

"Yes. Of course. But don't bother with stripping the thorns. She won't mind them."

Carmody followed her into the shop and seemed to leave his self-assurance in the back room. Silently he watched Rose bundle the roses into white paper tied with a scarlet ribbon.

She handed the bouquet to him. "I hope your aunt recovers and is able to celebrate her birthday in comfort."

He gravely accepted the bouquet. "I am certain these flowers will be much appreciated."

Their gazes met for the space of several heartbeats. An almost-smile quivered on his lips and Rose guessed he knew she was aware of his fabricated relative. Neither of them mentioned the ruse as he bid her good day and left the store.

Pain burned in her vinegar-anointed hand. A different sort of heat quickened her pulse as she watched from the window while her visitor strode down the street. She wasn't sure if she was flattered or distressed by his interest in her, but either way a strong interest in learning more about William Carmody grew.

Hattie might be able to answer some of her questions.

CHAPTER THREE

"THANK YOU FOR the lovely bouquet of roses, William, and for coming to visit. But, have you listened to a word I've said this past quarter hour?" Mother berated him over the third course of dinner.

"Yes, I have. But I've nothing to say on the matter," Will replied, as courteously as he could manage. She would not be happy with his answer, for all she wanted to hear was that he would further explore one of the marital prospects she suggested.

His mother set down her fork and offered her full regard. "Which means, I suppose, that you will *not* attend Lady Smyth's party and meet Miss Belinda Blake. You will not even make an attempt to enter social life, which you might find you enjoy after all." Her voice pitched higher as she concluded, "You will not befriend a fine young woman like Miss Belinda or her visiting cousin from Derby, Miss Elizabeth Chesterfield."

"Mother, would you have me agree to attend only to make an excuse and bow out later? For that is what will happen if you keep insisting. I do not enjoy these sorts of events or engaging in desultory conversation with women with whom I have nothing in common."

Unless the woman happened to be Miss Rose Gardener. He could not pinpoint what it was about her that had immediately seized his attention. It was not merely her pretty face, for he had seen plenty of those in his lifetime. There was something about her joyful demeanor, the way she carried herself, and how she spoke that attracted him beyond all reason. Will wanted to return to the shop simply to listen to her voice. She might speak on any subject and he would be enthralled.

Mother engaged Father in their argument. "Horace! Tell him he ought to go."

He looked up from his empty bowl with a gruff, "Hmph." His hazel eyes, a mirror of Will's own, darted back and forth between son and wife. "Best do as your mother bids. She is generally right about this sort of thing. It *is* time you were married and started a family. It's what one does… isn't it."

Will sighed. "Very well. I will attend Lady Smyth's party and meet these young ladies, but do not expect me to stay for long."

"A respectable length. You must dance and chat with each of them. Do make an effort, William." With her goal accomplished, his mother's harangue subsided, and she spoke more gently. "I comprehend your anxiety in social situations, dear. If you feel ill at ease, find a topic of interest to the lady and allow her to do the talking. It will remove the onus of carrying the conversation from you."

Good advice. He would be sure to apply it next time he went to the florist's. Rather than fumbling for something clever to say, he would discover a topic of interest to Miss Gardener. Guy had mentioned her devotion to the suffrage cause. That should do the trick. As it was a cause he agreed with, it should be easy to concur with what she said.

The rest of the meal passed uneventfully. As usual, Mother spoke of her garden club and her prize-winning roses. Will suggested she might try Rose Gardener's Florist for any supplies she might require for her hobby.

"Why in the world would I go all the way into the city, when everything I need is available in the village?"

Father suddenly interrupted. "Your mother wants the tennis court dug up and turned into a water garden. Rupert and Virginia don't care about anything other than their horses, but I thought you or Penelope might have an opinion as you both play on occasion."

"I'd prefer the court remain since Guy and I use it, but I don't live here. You've given me the London house for my own. That in itself is generous enough. Mother should do as she likes."

"Of course, you must have a say. I told you he would mind, Gwyneth. Find another spot to locate your pond."

"Waterscape," she corrected. "A profusion of fountains, one spilling into the next, and culminating in a pond with water lilies. But if William wants the court, naturally we shall keep it."

A passing thought galvanized him. "Mother, might I transplant one or two of your rosebushes to the conservatory in the London house?"

She laughed. "Don't be silly. One does not transplant fully mature bushes without risk of killing them. And the conservatory is in no condition to house anything. You must be aware the panes need glazing and a new radiator system ought to be installed. Good gracious, do you pay no attention to your surroundings?"

Truth be told, the most important room in the house was his precious library, which he had expanded into an adjacent room to house his collection. Will had hardly noticed the conservatory falling into disrepair. After having electricity installed throughout the house, he'd neglected any further home improvements.

"I'm afraid I have been derelict in my duties. I haven't cared for the house as well as I ought. I shall do better."

Beginning with the conservatory. Tomorrow he would hire workers to bring it up to snuff then ask Miss Gardener for advice on filling it with growing things. He would create an opportunity to communicate with her often for a legitimate reason.

Eager to drive home and begin planning, Will pushed his chair away from the table. "I am sorry. I shan't be able to stay for a game of whist this evening. Do you mind?"

His mother's eyes widened. "Good heavens, we haven't yet finished our meal. Cook made your favorite dessert. It would be too unkind to disappoint her."

So Will remained, hardly tasting one mouthful of the lemon merengue that had been his favorite as a child. Perhaps he might plant a lemon or orange tree in the conservatory. He could almost smell citrus trees growing safe under glass in the dead of winter. Horticulture had just become his new passion. He would dive deeply into the books he'd recently purchased so he might speak intelligently with Miss Gardener.

It wasn't until he had driven home and entered the silence of his bachelor house that Will paused to consider the reasoning behind his new venture. Did he honestly believe Miss Gardener would become enamored of him simply because he asked her a few questions about plants? She was a beautiful young woman and he a stodgy bookworm, hardly the romantic hero of a girl's fancy. The pair of them together would be like an ostrich with a dove—ridiculous and improbable.

Miss Gardener might help him acquire plants for the greenhouse, but that was all. Better to forget the way her bright smile lit his dark spaces. Time to stop imagining how that fiery hair that Guy pretended had burned him would feel like to the touch. Soft as the skin of her hand, no doubt. He imagined glossy tendrils sliding between his fingers and sparkling blue eyes regarding him with affection. Such a sweet dream must ever remain a fantasy.

Heaving a glum sigh, Will changed into night attire then settled into an armchair to read. An old favorite, *The Life of Galileo* beckoned him, but instead, he studied one of the new volumes he had purchased: *The Science of Horticulture*. Regardless of whether he contacted Miss Gardener or not, he had promised Mother to refurbish the conservatory. At least one corner of his barren house would be filled with vibrant life.

CHAPTER FOUR

As Rose paid her supplier for the day's delivery, she considered what she would do when winter came. The price of hothouse blooms was exorbitant. It would be wonderful if she could raise at least some flowers in a glass lean-to or cold frame behind the building. But she could not afford something like that, even if her landlord or the zoning laws permitted it.

She walked from the delivery door into the shop, head down, lost in a daydream in which flowers were plentiful and always in perfect bloom.

"Pardon me, Miss Gardener," a low male voice interrupted her thoughts. Though she had heard only a handful of sentences spoken by that voice, she already recognized it.

Rose offered the speaker a welcoming smile. "Good morning, Mr. Carmody. How may I help you today?"

He remained near the door, careful not to take her by surprise again and far away from any obstructions, holding his hat in hand. "I am here for two reasons, Miss Gardener. One is to procure a bouquet. The other is to discuss a proposition."

His second statement put her on guard. She had been propositioned by groping tossers in her old neighborhood and by lads at the dance hall where she and the other boarding house girls would go on a Saturday evening. Even gentlemanly customers had sometimes murmured scandalous invitations.

"I will gladly assemble a bouquet for you," she replied primly. "What sort of flowers?"

"Lilies, if you have them. Or anything. It doesn't matter. What I'm mostly interested in is your advice on the renovation of my conservatory. I've hired a glazier to repair the panes, but I know very little about plants and their needs. I had hoped you might come to my house to observe the progress of the restoration and make some suggestions on what flora I should choose."

Come over indeed. As if she were the sort of woman who would stop by a single man's house. Although, Carmody had been very courtly while treating her thorn wound. She rubbed the spot, recalling the feel of his warm hand cupping hers. The slight tingle there must be from the healing process.

It was certainly serendipitous that Mr. Carmody should request her advice on a topic she'd been considering mere seconds before. It felt like some sort of message from on high.

"Since you mention the subject, Mr. Carmody, I was just now thinking of indoor gardening and how it might be managed in our cold and overcast English winter. However, I must warn you that I am no expert on growing plants by any means. I depend on a book I bought to educate me on the subject: *The Science of Horticulture*."

Her visitor's eyes widened. "I recently purchased the same volume and was just reading it last night."

She laughed in delight. "Perhaps we might study together and exchange our thoughts on what we learn. I would be pleased to have a fellow botany enthusiast with whom to discuss plants." Rose blurted the invitation without thinking of how it might sound.

Carmody paused. Perhaps he thought her offer too forward. But then he replied, "Yes. I would be amenable to that at any time that would be convenient for you. Also, I would greatly appreciate your view on the repairs to my conservatory."

"I would enjoy seeing it very much, but I should not visit a bachelor's home without a chaperone."

"Of course not." He dropped his gaze, adjusted his spectacles, then peered at her with bright eyes. "Perhaps if both your friend and mine were present, it would be suitable? I shall arrange a dinner party and viewing of the work in progress."

"That would be all right. Whenever you wish to arrange it, I will—"

A customer arrived to interrupt her thought. Rose turned her attention to the woman in a blue gown and matching plumed hat, which Rose recognized as one of Hattie's. "Good day. Welcome to my shop. May I help you with anything in particular?"

The woman shot a look between Rose and Mr. Carmody. "I will browse while you finish serving your customer."

"After you, Madam," Carmody said. "I must choose an appropriate bereavement note." He stepped toward the display.

The flustered woman required several centerpieces for a tea she was hosting that very day. "I completely forgot about flowers. There's nothing to cut in the garden, and now, I've left it so late I haven't the time to arrange them myself. Could you make four centerpieces and deliver them before two today?"

The close deadline seemed nearly unachievable. Still, Rose could not bear to turn down any order. "Pink roses and white gardenias," she repeated the woman's request. "I have both on hand."

After her harried customer had left, Rose exclaimed aloud, "What have I done?"

Mr. Carmody replaced the card he pretended to study. "Will you be unable to complete the order in time?"

"I should be able to, but not with interruptions from customers. Guy is right. I need an assistant, if only for a few hours each day." She recalled to whom she was speaking. "Never mind my worries. Let me make your bouquet."

"There is no special occasion. I'll buy them another time. You must begin filling that order. Might I offer to watch the store for you? I am not experienced, but I believe I could greet customers and do my best to help them."

She couldn't have been more shocked if he'd offered to get down on his knees and scrub the floors. "I couldn't possibly ask such a favor of you."

"You wouldn't want to disappoint a new customer. It would be bad for business." He studied her with translucent eyes which shaded toward leaf-green in the light. "You are a friend of Hardy's and therefore a friend of mine. Allow me to help you as he would."

Rose dipped her head, his keen gaze making her feel unaccountably shy and shaky. Of course he had no inappropriate designs on her, but was merely looking out for her on his friend's behalf. "I would greatly appreciate your help. Thank you, Mr. Carmody. I will work as quickly as I can, and if you need help with a customer, you must summon me from the back room."

"I certainly will." He gave a small bow as naturally as breathing. The men in Rose's life did not bow. She didn't come from that sort of people. His courtesy and the way he looked at her through the clear glass shield of his spectacles made her shaky, trembling feeling grow.

Now *she* was the one with inappropriate thoughts! Banishing them, Rose bustled around the shop collecting flowers, the strong fragrance of the gardenias nearly overwhelming the equally powerful scent of roses. Perhaps the pairing was too fragrant for a tea table, but they would certainly look beautiful together.

At her worktable, Rose placed four shallow ceramic bowls with a metal frog in each. She stripped leaves and thorns from stems and placed each bloom. The arrangement grew from sparse into an explosion of pink and white blossoms anchored in green ferns. As she examined the first finished centerpiece, a glow of pride filled her. Her flowers were every bit as artistic as Hattie's couture creations. Not bad for a factory girl who only dreamed of creating something so lovely as she plucked an endless line of dead chickens in a cannery.

Rose peeked through the curtains into the shop. There were no customers, so Mr. Carmody had taken it upon himself to prune dead bits from the potted plants. Unaware of her watching, he moved with considerably more grace than usual, circling and snipping assuredly. What had made an educated, titled, wealthy fellow like William Carmody so insecure? It was a puzzle, and Rose dearly loved solving those.

As if feeling her gaze, Carmody began to turn. Rose retreated behind the curtain, heart bumping a trifle too fast, and returned to her work.

Sometime later, four almost perfectly matched arrangements stood in a row. After admiring them a moment, she went to telephone her delivery man. God bless Guy for insisting on installing the wondrous invention in both her business and Hattie's. The modern tool made life so much easier.

In the shop, Rose found Mr. Carmody besieged by customers. She joined him in serving the rush. For the next twenty minutes, flowers flew out the door, the full buckets diminishing and orders for arrangements "like the attractive one in the window" rising.

Rose rejoiced over every sale, although she began to fear she had not bought enough stock. It was difficult to calculate how many flowers would be needed on any given day. Growing things were more trouble than the silk flowers, ribbons and laces at the millinery. Those might go out of fashion but would never fade or decay so one could keep a generous supply on hand.

When the shop was empty once more, Rose leaned against the counter with a sigh.

Mr. Carmody sat down heavily on the stool. "Is it always so busy? How do you manage on your own?"

"Sometimes it is difficult, but I can't really afford to hire an assistant yet. I cannot thank you enough for your aid today. You stepped in and did precisely what was needed."

His gaze dropped. "I was happy to help. Were you able to finish your order in time?"

"The delivery man arrived in back while you were occupied. I suppose my customers thought it odd a fine gentleman was assisting them."

"They did not look past the apron." He indicated her striped apron which he had donned. It was ludicrously short on his long form. "Anyway, I'm the sort of fellow people don't notice, which is fine with me as I prefer to blend into the wallpaper."

"I feel the same way," Rose said. "I prefer to blend in and remain unnoticed."

Carmody rose from the stool. "Miss Gardener, I don't believe you could avoid being seen. Your appearance invites attention. Your hair... and your eyes. You are like..." He mutely waved his hands as if performing a magic trick. "You are a lightning flash."

Embarrassment etched a scarlet trail across her cheeks. "Oh my! You are too kind. That is the most, er, descriptive compliment I have ever received."

He wedged his hands into the apron pockets and looked out the window.

Rose wished to soothe his perpetual discomfort. "*You* could never blend into the wallpaper, Mr. Carmody. Your presence is *indomitable.* I think that is the word I mean. Strong and resolute. Is that correct?"

"That is how you perceive me?"

"Yes. Absolutely. A rock, someone on whom a person may rely." She extended her hand, inviting a shake. "Might I consider you a friend, Mr. Carmody?"

"I hope you will, Miss Gardener, for I should very much like to be yours."

They formally shook, once... twice, before letting go.

"I must leave now, as I have a tutoring appointment this afternoon," he said.

Guy had never mentioned his friend taught, another facet of this unusual Mr. Carmody to explore. "I pray helping me has not made you late."

"Not at all." Carmody met her gaze with piercing eyes and a subdued smile. "Good day, Miss Gardener."

"Good day, Mr. Carmody."

Rose watched him leave and touched together the fingers of the hand he had shaken. She assured herself the reason she felt a bit lightheaded and swoony was because she had not eaten any lunch.

What a difference a few hours could make. That morning she had dreamed of a greenhouse and the prospect of designing one had dropped into her lap. She had wished for help in the shop and a courteous man arrived to aid her. Like the fortuitous first meeting with Hattie at the bookstore, when they had spoken of business and Hattie hired Rose as her assistant, what other unexpected turns of events might be in store in this wonderful life?

CHAPTER FIVE

THE FOLLOWING EVENING Rose received a thick, cream-colored envelope with her name and address written in fine slanting script—an invitation to Mr. William Carmody's home for a dinner party and conservatory viewing. Rose brought the message to her nose and inhaled the papery scent of fine stationery, but no whiff of the man's subtle cologne.

It was not late, so she hurried down the street to the millinery, praying Hattie was at home and not visiting her fiancé. Her friend opened the side door and Rose entered the work room where she had spent so many hours sewing decorations on hats.

Released from its Gibson roll, Hattie's chestnut hair fell loose around her shoulders. Rose too had removed her hairpins and shook her hair free as soon as the last customer of the day was gone. Only women could know the discomfort one went through for fashion's sake.

Hattie embraced Rose with affection—the sort of hug that Rose and her sister Arietta had never shared. "Here we are, only a few shops apart, and I feel as if I never see you. We must make a pact to eat lunch together at least once weekly. I could come to yours since I have Margaret now to look after my shop. How are you managing without an assistant?"

Rose removed her hat and gloves. "I had one yesterday. Guy's friend William Carmody, of all people. He stopped by to discuss his conservatory renovation and stayed to wait on customers while I filled an unexpected order."

"So *that* is what this dinner invitation is about. I wondered what on earth incited Will to arrange a dinner party. It is so unlike him."

"Is it? I know scarcely anything about the man and hoped you might fill in some details."

Hattie's dimples flashed. "Certainly. Come upstairs where we may sit comfortably, and I'll tell you what little I know about Mr. Carmody."

The layout of Hattie's flat was similar to Rose's, but the décor was nothing alike. Rose had bought whatever pieces of used furniture she could afford, hiding their flaws under brightly colored paint. Potted plants filled nooks and crannies, covering peeling wallpaper. She adored the homey atmosphere of the first space she had ever called her own. In contrast, Hattie's formerly Spartan rooms now glowed with muted pastels and elegantly carved furniture in a style called Art Nouveau. Guy's influence without a doubt, yet the tone reflected Hattie's taste as well.

Rose sat at the small table while Hattie prepared a fresh pot of tea.

"I don't believe Will has spoken more than a handful of words to me since we met. But it sounds as if he's taken a shine to you," Hattie teased.

"Bosh! He simply wanted to ask what sort of plants to put in his greenhouse." But of course, Hattie was right. A man didn't show up on pretexts of buying flowers or asking horticulture questions if he wasn't at least a little interested. The knowledge gave Rose a tingle of excitement and unease. "So, tell me all you know about him."

Hattie leaned against the counter. "As you may have noticed, Mr. Carmody is shy, particularly around women. He is very well-read. Guy says the man has more books in his personal collection than there are in the London Library, and may be counted on to answer questions on nearly any topic. A walking encyclopedia."

"Is he a professor? He mentioned meeting a student."

"He tutors university students who are struggling with their studies, particularly scholarship students without funds to pay a tutor. He comes from a well-respected lineage. His parents are Lord Horace and Lady Gwyneth Carmody. His elder brother Rupert will inherit the estate, so the family has apparently given Will their London home and the freedom to do as he likes." Hattie paused. "I believe there is a younger sister, but I've forgotten her name. Is this the sort of information you're seeking?"

Rose nodded, disappointment blooming. She'd known his station was far above hers, but mention of an ancestral estate only served to remind her they were worlds apart. Any notion of romance was impossible, other than something short-lived and tawdry. He was not for the likes of her.

Hattie set a cup and saucer in front of Rose and spoke as if reading her mind, "William Carmody is not a cad. He is too gentlemanly to toy with a woman's affections or make unwanted advances. I believe he is quite lonely and tired of solitude, although he would not say so. Clearly, he enjoys your company and that is sufficient. At any rate, Guy and I will be at hand to ease any awkwardness at this dinner."

"I could not go without you there." Rose cradled her steaming cup. "Now tell me, what is happening with your wedding plans? Will you set a date soon?"

Hattie gave her a sharp look. "Did Guy tell you to ask me that?"

"Heavens, no! I only ask because I am interested in your plans. Why? Are you having second thoughts about marrying him?"

Her friend exhaled and leaned back in her seat. "No second thoughts. Of course I want to marry him. I love the silly devil. But something holds me back from setting a date. I'm not quite sure what it is."

Knowing about the great heartbreak that had damaged Hattie at a young age, Rose guessed she might know the answer. "Do you trust in Guy's affection for you?"

"Yes. I do."

"You believe his feelings will not alter and he would never stray from you in the future?"

Hattie's habitual calm ruffled and she shifted nervously. "He had many lovers before we met. How do I know he would not lapse into old ways some day?"

"Because it is *Guy*! However he may have behaved before, he is not the same man now. He loves you beyond all reason and would never betray you. I feel that in my heart." Rose pressed her palm to her chest. "Besides, he knows if he ever hurt you in any way, I'd take a butcher knife to the part of him that did the straying."

Hattie choked on a sip of tea as she laughed. "I believe you would." Then she sobered. "I must admit, I don't actually worry about putting my trust in him. What I fear is losing my freedom. I own a shop, work every day, and have my own flat to retire to. No matter how forward-thinking Guy's views on female emancipation, I fear I might become simply a wife with expected duties. Perhaps he will wish me to work less and devote more time to running our household. As for children, I'm not quite sure—"

"That you are ready," Rose completed her thought.

Rose recalled how her mother had scolded her for refusing the Goggins boy at age sixteen. *His dad's a butcher. You'll never have to pluck another bleedin' chicken unless it's for your own stewpot. Chances like this don't come along every day, girl. Soon you'll lose that pretty face and figure, and end up wed to some mangy fellow who drinks away his paycheck.* Mum had shot a long-suffering look at her husband.

Although Rose had been fond of the lad and certainly enjoyed kissing him, she was wise enough to know she was not in love with him. Choosing to marry must mean a great deal more than finding a way out of the cannery, she had known even at a young age. Lifelong commitment required a great deal of sacrifice.

"I understand," Rose continued. "Our friend Mr. Hardy must simply remain patient until you are ready to commit to a date."

Hattie nodded. "That is precisely what I want, but recently whenever we are together, even if he doesn't mention the subject, I feel it in the air between us. Soon I must address the issue, for we can't go on like this forever." She paused. "And I *do* want to marry him and share a home. I truly do, but..."

"You aren't quite ready," Rose repeated.

Hattie smiled widely. "You do understand. Thank you for listening to my fears."

"That's what friends do, and I will always be here to share your troubles with you." Rose changed the subject. "Now, tell me, what sort of gown is appropriate to wear to a fancy dinner party?"

"I will find you something in my closet, for we are of a like size." Hattie eyed Rose critically. "I've just made the sweetest, smartest hat that would suit your hair and complexion perfectly."

HOURS LATER, ROSE returned to her shop with a beaded blue gown in a box, a pair of satin slippers to match, and a tiny feathered creation to top off the ensemble. As she climbed the stairs to her flat, she considered what Hattie had told her about Carmody.

He might be a kind and respectful gentleman as Hattie had said, but in Rose's experience lads who liked her looks always pushed for more. They could not seem to keep their hands to themselves. Hattie was a bit naïve if she believed Carmody would remain content with polite friendship. He likely craved something more physical than conversation.

It was up to Rose to decide if she cared to give it to him. A part of her imagined those large, competent hands gliding over her body and thought that she might like to.

CHAPTER SIX

As Rose rode the tram across the city to attend the WSPU meeting the next evening, anticipation and nerves over the upcoming supper party waltzed together through her brain. Tonight's meeting should distract her from her excitement and fears. Rose had offered to supply floral arrangements to the proposed Women's Parliament, and already envisioned them. But a sub-committee must discuss every detail of hall decoration as if it were as important as the rally and march itself.

Once again, the dark-haired woman from the other night slipped into a chair beside her.

"Miss Violet," Rose greeted her. "I'm very glad you decided to come back. Are you feeling any better?"

The girl seemed embarrassed by her teary state during their first meeting. "I apologize for my outburst. I wasn't feeling quite myself." Her modulated tone reminded Rose of a cello solo she'd heard once in a park pavilion concert, lovely, but with an undernote of melancholy that touched the heart.

"Allow me to introduce myself again," she continued. "My name is Candace Sweet. I felt the need to hide my identity, but I wish to be honest with you, Miss Gardener." Doe eyes regarded her with uncertainty.

"You may trust me with your true name. No suffragette would

ever reveal who they may have seen at one of the meetings. There could be dire consequences for some. Many are here despite their family's disapproval. I fear driving away my customers should they learn I support suffrage. We all do what we must and aide the cause within our capability."

"It was quite difficult for me to get away, and it comforts me to know others face the same challenge," Miss Sweet confided.

The chair of her committee interrupted their conversation. "Miss Gardener, will you be able to get as many as five dozen white and red roses?"

"It may be difficult," Rose replied. "Refrigeration is the issue. Has anyone access to a large icebox?"

For the next twenty minutes, discussion over refrigeration, renting chairs and hanging bunting wore on until finally the meeting ended.

Rose's new friend touched her elbow lightly. "Miss Gardener, might we speak privately?"

"Of course, Miss Sweet. My shop is but a tram ride away."

"I haven't much time. I must return home before I am missed." She watched the dispersing suffragettes and whispered urgently, "But if I do not talk with someone I shall go mad. I have no one in whom I may confide."

Rose recalled her heartfelt conversation in Hattie's kitchen the previous evening. Such unburdening was vital to a person. "Whatever you tell me I will hold in the strictest confidence. Have you come here by cab? We might walk together to the nearest stand."

"I would appreciate that very much."

Out on the street, the WSPU members dispersed in various directions. The fashionable neighborhood was well-lit by electric street lamps. Rose and her new friend passed from one pool of light to another as they strolled. Miss Sweet's constraint had returned, and Rose finally prompted her to speak.

"Is it a problem in your family?" She recalled Jennifer Pruett's difficulties and how Hattie had aided her. "An unwanted match perhaps?"

"Something of the sort, although no offer of marriage has yet been made. But I feel he is on the brink of it, and I don't know how I may reject him or his … attentions. He is the only thing close to family that I have." Miss Sweet bit her lip. "Oh, this is so difficult to say."

"Whatever you tell me, I will not judge you." To set Miss Sweet at ease, Rose offered her own history. "I come from Spitalfields. I improved my speech and manners and found better employment, eventually opening my shop. But I forever hear my family's voices saying I'm not good enough, that I'm acting above myself, that I will be found out and my enterprise will fail. A dear friend convinced me I am worthy of being where I am today, yet sometimes those childhood voices are louder. Trust me when I say I will listen to you with an open mind."

Miss Sweet had stopped walking. Light illuminated half of her face. The rest was cast in shadow. She swallowed before speaking.

"My guardian took me in after my parents died of influenza when I was very young. Since my return from school in Paris, he has begun looking at me with…." She shook her head. "That is not quite true. Even before I left for school at age thirteen, the feeling that he observed me in a peculiar way began. His gaze was not at all polite or paternal. Do you understand?"

"I have an uncle who would give me *that* sort of a look. Nothing came of it beyond some too familiar pats on the backside, but I do understand. Has this man made any improper suggestions?"

Candace shook her head. "But I feel it is only a matter of time. He assures me I needn't worry about having a debutante season because he already has a husband in mind for me—a mature man who will guard me, guide me, and attend to all of my needs. The implication is that he is referring to himself."

Miss Sweet pressed her palms to her stomach as if illustrating the spot from which her suspicions rose, or attempting to suppress queasiness. "I am almost twenty. If I can but hold him off until I reach the age of majority, I will gain control of my inheritance and my freedom. But I feel quite certain this man will not allow that."

"He desires you *and* your fortune," Rose said.

Miss Sweet nodded. "Every instinct tells me to run away before I am backed into a corner and cannot escape. But without a reference, it would be difficult to gain employment. My godfather has always paid for my needs, and never allowed me more than a little pocket money. I have saved a little, but am still as financially helpless as a child. Much as I would love to be brave like the suffragettes who go to prison for their cause, I don't know if I could survive on my own without a penny."

"Living in this world ain't… isn't easy," Rose agreed. "I worked at a factory since age ten. Even with my whole family pitching in, life was hard."

Partly because Mum drank away what was due to the landlord and Dad bought beer rather than bread.

"You should have your inheritance," Rose declared emphatically. "Why should you abandon it to this snake? There must be a way to state your case in court."

Miss Sweet exhaled and turned so shadow completely obscured her face. "If there is, I haven't the wherewithal to hire legal counsel. I don't know how long I can stall Mr. Merker, but I fear a wedding will take place before my twenty-first birthday. Should I refuse, he would find a way to drive me to the altar."

"I wish I knew of some way to help you. I will try to think of something, but meanwhile, you may visit me at my shop any time you wish to talk, or if you are in fear for your safety."

Tears welled in Miss Sweet's eyes and spilled down her cheeks. Her shoulders shook as she pressed her hand to her mouth to hold back a sob.

Rose rested a hand on her back. "There now. You'll be all right.

Together we will find a way. I have a friend who might recommend a solicitor."

After regaining her composure, Miss Sweet spoke again. "You cannot know how much it means to me to have a friend to talk with about such a personal matter. My schoolmates at Madame Brodeur's Académie are scattered far and wide, nor is this a topic I could have discussed with them. We were sheep taught to be obedient, pleasant and polite, perfect young women preparing to become perfect wives. Any one of those friends would advise me to listen to what my guardian suggests, for he must have my best interests at heart."

"Bollocks! Those girls sound like bleedin' idiots." Rose lost her polish entirely.

Miss Sweet's eyes widened and her mouth dropped open. Then she began to laugh, a soft chuckle which turned into a gale of laughter verging on hysteria.

Rose grinned. "Feeling better?"

Her new friend gasped for breath. "Yes, I do. Much better. Thank you, Miss Gardener. Your descriptive words express everything that is in my heart in such a refreshingly honest manner."

A cab had stopped at the stand where they waited. Rose impulsively drew the young woman into a swift hug. "If ever things become too dire, you must promise to come to me for help, Miss Sweet."

"Please, call me Candace. I think we've moved beyond formalities, don't you? Thank you again for listening to me."

"We women must support each other, for those louts who blunder around trying to control our lives never will."

Candace waved goodbye and stepped into the waiting taxi.

Rose watched the vehicle drive away. She had not expected the evening to take such a strange turn. Candace's story had certainly served to drive trifling worries about a dinner party from her mind. She might not know the girl very well, but sharing a familiar feeling of belittlement had bonded them. Rose had found a kindred spirit in the soft-spoken young lady with the sad brown eyes.

CHAPTER SEVEN

WILL STUDIED THE dining room table. The only new thing upon its surface was an arrangement of fresh flowers, purchased from another florist since it would be strange to have Miss Gardener make the centerpiece for a party she attended. Every other item was ancient, from the linen tablecloth and napkins to the silver plate, china, and glasses featuring the Carmody family crest. Even though the cutlery and glassware were polished to a shine, the overall impression was old-fashioned and dull.

Nearly all the furniture in the townhouse was a century old. Will had done little to modernize, beyond installing electricity and converting the room adjoining the library into an annex for more books. The idea of refreshing the décor hadn't occurred to him until this moment, when he observed the place as Rose might when she arrived in less than half an hour.

Will had dressed earlier, but hurried to his room to review his reflection in the dressing room mirror. Like Guy, he eschewed the services of a valet, so he stood alone, gazing at himself and realizing there was little he could do to change his looks. He had tamed his wavy locks with a wet comb since he couldn't bear the slick feeling of hair oil, and already his hair flopped about at will. Why hadn't he sought a barber for a trim?

At least his suit was new. His tailor had been thrilled to outfit him in a modern double-breasted suit jacket with narrow lapels. Will appeared more like stylish Guy, and less like some hermit uncle emerging from an attic in a decade-old jacket.

He forced himself to draw his shoulders back. Guy had advised him to take advantage of his height rather than slump to hide it. "Ladies love a fellow who appears confident. You wish to make a good impression on Miss Gardener, don't you?"

"I don't intend to impress her. I only seek her advice on the best plants for the conservatory. This dinner party is to ensure her visit will be properly chaperoned."

"Ah, I see, so you wouldn't be at all tempted to kiss her if the opportunity arose," Guy had teased.

Rather than slap the smirk off his friend's face, Will had kept quiet.

But a seed once planted would grow, and ever since those words were spoken, his active brain envisioned various scenarios that might end in a kiss.

He settled his spectacles on his nose, for he couldn't see well enough to get by without them, and stared at himself again. His eyes were enlarged and the glasses only brought attention to his big nose. The man in the mirror shook his head. Hopeless. No kisses would ever be coming his way, so he might as well erase such imaginings from his mind.

With only minutes before his guests' arrival, Will sat in the drawing room with the compendium on horticulture opened to a random page. His stomach flipped when the doorbell rang, and he listened to Reardon welcome his guests.

At the sound of approaching footsteps, he resumed staring at the book as if fascinated. His pulse raced, but he waited until Reardon announced the guests before setting the book aside and rising to greet them.

"Welcome! So good of you to come. Do sit down."

Hardy handed off a bottle of wine for Reardon to pour them an aperitif. "Happy to be here, old chap, and looking forward to seeing the improvements on the conservatory."

"Your home is charming," Miss Glover said. "Thank you for the dinner invitation."

Will was already at ease with the woman who had transformed Hardy from an aimless bachelor into a purposeful man. Hattie's smile helped settle his nerves.

But then he looked at Miss Gardener and his wits fled completely. She was stunning. A deep blue gown made her eyes even brighter. The bodice framed her neck and shoulders, modest yet emphasizing her curves. Her high-piled red hair sported a charming concoction of blue netting and a few feathers. If he could nuzzle just at the corner of her jaw where sparkling earrings dangled, all his dreams would be fulfilled.

He gulped and spoke, "Your dress is most becoming, Miss Gardener."

"Thank you, Mr. Carmody. I feel rather a sham. I will admit I have never been to a fancy dinner party before."

How could one not fall a little in love with a woman so unabashedly honest, a curious mixture of confidence and insecurity? He wanted to say he was happy to host her first such event, but couldn't think of a way to say it without sounding condescending. So he simply nodded mutely.

Luckily, Reardon interrupted the silence with the tray of glasses.

After the butler withdrew from the room, Guy raised his glass. "A toast to old and new friendships, and to unexpected changes that bring great reward."

"Well said." Hattie regarded Guy with such a pure expression of love that Will felt as if he witnessed a private moment. He looked away and met Miss Gardener's gaze. She winked at him, uniting them outside the lovebirds' private bubble.

Will swallowed too fast and choked on his wine.

"Have we time before the meal to view the conservatory, Mr.

Carmody?" she asked. "I very much look forward to seeing it."

"Of course."

Will led the way toward the back of the house, already making excuses for the work in progress. "The glazier has begun his work so the panes are smeared with putty, but he will clean them before he is through. Next week a free-standing radiator will be installed. Beyond that, I require your assistance, Miss Gardener, for I'm certain you will be better than I at creating an attractive design."

He looked at the lovely woman walking beside him, a waft of her perfume teasing his senses.

"You give me too much credit. I am only beginning to learn about the varieties of plants that thrive in a greenhouse. You could find an expert to better advise you."

"No! That is, I prefer to work on the project with another novice. I wouldn't want someone who takes over the project. Besides which, I admire your eye for design."

"Indeed," Guy backed him. "You are the woman for the job, Rose. Isn't she, darling?"

"Absolutely," Hattie agreed. "She will help you create a veritable Garden of Eden."

They passed through the library annex, and Will opened the double doors leading into the conservatory. Muted sunlight shone through smudged glass panes outlined in weathered wood. The replacement panes were much clearer than the older ones, but at least the ceiling and walls were intact once more.

Slatted tables on which his mother had once arranged cut flowers sat empty. Will rapped on one. "The wood is decayed and fragile so these will need replacing. I thought I might have low beds installed, perhaps with an orange tree in that corner so I might have fresh citrus in winter. What do you think, Miss Gardener? Could one survive a cloudy English winter?"

Will knew the answer, having read it in the horticulture book.

Citrus thrived in England under proper growing conditions. But he awaited his guest's response.

Rose nodded. "You mentioned your interest, so I read up on caring for potted citrus trees. They will remain in an outdoor garden until autumn, when one must gradually introduce them to the greenhouse climate. With proper soil, moisture, and light, they will bear fruit."

"Come, Guy. Let us step into the library and look through the books while these two discuss greenery." Hattie took her fiancé's arm and drew him into the neighboring room.

It seemed obvious she was creating privacy for Will and Miss Gardener, but if the young lady felt ill at ease, she showed no sign.

Rose stood with an elbow resting on one folded arm, chin on fist, and regarded the space with a charming frown. "Have you considered raising herbs as well? I thought perhaps a small bed close to the inner wall to provide easy access for your kitchen staff. But this is such a small space, perhaps you do not wish to use any of it on a kitchen garden."

"I am open to all possibilities. My housekeeper cooks for me as well. She might appreciate fresh herbs."

"Have you a blueprint for the room? Knowing the dimensions could help in making the best possible use of every square foot. We could pencil in possible designs and just as quickly change them."

"I will supply you with a copy that you may draw on to your heart's content," he promised. Her enthusiasm for the project ignited his own fervor—not only for the plan but for the planner.

Miss Gardener walked around the room, examining the rotted wood tables, then stooping to gather a handful of soil and allowing it to sift through her fingers. "Do you prefer plants with a strong fragrance or something more muted? I was considering night blooming jasmine. They have a powerfully sweet odor, which some find cloying. But the white blossoms would be lovely in the moonlight contrasted against the dark green leaves of the orange tree."

Her face would be lovely in the moonlight.

"I'm certain it would be beautiful. Whatever you wish to do, I concur."

"But it's *your* conservatory. I want to make certain you enjoy sitting here, perhaps reading a book on a small bench." She turned slowly. "Can you imagine frost on the panes, a cold wind whistling outside, as you enjoy an abundance of greenery on a winter's night?"

"I can feel it exactly as you've described." A nearly forgotten memory resurfaced and he found himself sharing it. "I recall sitting on the ground playing with marbles while my mother tended her roses. She still raises hybrid varieties, some of which she created herself."

He touched the rickety table. "She would hum off-key as rain beat against the glass. On the ground, I aimed my marbles and distinctly remember the soft, satisfying *click* as one connected with another, sending it shooting off. I had quite forgotten that snug and perfectly content feeling."

Rose made a soft hum of appreciation. "That sounds heavenly. I wish I had had such a fond memory from my childhood." She glanced around as if wondering how the place had fallen into such disrepair. "So, your mother is an expert gardener."

"Yes. She personally oversees the garden staff at Carmody Hall. Roses are her particular passion, and one of her varieties placed in a national competition."

"Why would you not simply ask for her suggestions on what to plant?"

Why indeed? He scrambled to invent an answer. "My parents prefer living year-round in the country, so they offered the townhouse to me. My elder brother Rupert, who will inherit the estate, is not at all interested in London society and agreed with this decision. As much as I adore Mother and admire her green thumb, I wish to make my own decisions about this house."

"It is *your* home now." Rose nodded. "But the house is quite large for one person. Do you never feel lonely here?"

She did not seem to consider the impertinence of the question, another example of her pure honesty.

"I am often so involved in my reading I could be anywhere on earth and not notice what is around me. I am a solitary person by nature. Yet, recently when I put my books aside, I become aware that the once soothing quietness seems arid and empty."

Embarrassed by his revelation, Will studied a beetle crawling across the floor.

"One may feel such loneliness even in a crowd," Rose replied. "I come from a very loud family living in a very small space. There was never a lack of people nearby, yet I often felt as if I lived on an ice floe, such as Admiral Peary describes in articles about exploring the far north. In the midst of chaos, I felt utterly alone. It wasn't until I met Miss Glover that I found a kindred spirit. She was my mentor as well as employer, and is now my dearest friend."

"I cannot imagine anyone as friendly as you feeling lonely. You are a bright, shining soul who attracts everyone around her like a flower draws honeybees."

A wry smile twisted her lips. "That is kind of you to say, but you haven't met my family. With them I am considered an outsider, an 'odd duck' as my mum often said. Their interest in me extended as far as the money I brought home from my job. Mum assured me I could never succeed in owning my own business." She stopped speaking, ducking her head in embarrassment. "I'm sorry. I've spoken too freely. You couldn't possibly be interested in my family woes."

"I am!" Will exclaimed. "I am interested in everything about you, Miss Gardener. Although I am quite hopeless at expressing my thoughts, I must tell you I wish to know you better. I pray you won't find my attention off-putting."

Prolonged silence followed, so thick one could spread it like marmalade. Will wished he could join the beetle, which had disappeared into a crack. He'd made a fool of himself by speaking so openly, veering like a wind vane from nearly mute to revealing far too much about his feelings.

"Mr. Carmody, I must admit to feeling flattered by your words, although I'm not sure what I've done to deserve them. I'm merely a common girl from Spitalfields with nothing special to recommend me. I am not on a par with you in any way." Rose added gently, "I would like to be your friend, but I believe it is best we maintain a professional distance while working on your conservatory project."

"Yes, of course." Will quickly backpedaled, humiliated that she now knew his romantic intent. "Your friendship would be sufficient. I would never expect more than that."

He inhaled slowly, burying his disappointment. If he did not quickly change the tone of the conversation, an excruciating evening lay before them. "Tell me more about this night-blooming jasmine. I am intrigued."

Rose plunged into the subject with apparent relief. "Outdoors, they may grow as high as eight feet with a circumference of three feet, but potting and pruning will keep them from taking up too much space. Still, I know you are more interested in the citrus trees, so they must be our first priority with all other plantings serving to complement them."

Before Will could ask further questions, Reardon arrived to announce supper. Will offered to escort Rose to the table, trying not to thrill at the touch of her hand on his arm.

In the library annex, Guy and Hattie joined their walk toward the dining room from which delicious scents wafted.

"You must show Rose your books after the meal," Hattie said. "What a widely varied collection."

"What subjects are of special interest to you, Mr. Carmody?" Rose enquired.

"I am particularly partial to books about the lives of daring explorers or forward-thinking scientists such as Galileo. Also any sort of history. One feels a greater connection to all that went before."

"History certainly makes one aware of the brevity of life," Guy chimed in as he held Hattie's chair. "One must seize the day whenever possible. No point in postponing important matters." He patted Hattie's shoulders before taking his seat.

The suggestion beneath his words was obvious. Will knew Hardy eagerly awaited a matrimonial date, which his betrothed seemed reluctant to set.

Rose must know it too, because she diverted the conversation. "What lovely table settings. Your home is so—" *Antiquated, ancient,* Will thought. "—impressive. I feel as if I've stepped back in time."

Rose seemed enchanted rather than dismayed by the venerable décor. "This chandelier is breathtaking." She gazed at the fixture draped with crystal pendants suspended above the table.

The pale column of her throat made Will's breath catch.

"One of my forebears brought it from France during the Seven Years' War. Of course it was never wired for gas lights, let alone electric, so it is never used."

"I can imagine the glory of it with all the candles lit."

When she dropped her gaze to his, Will wished he'd bothered to have the chandelier polished to a shine and fresh candles lit. If the glow would please her, it would be worth the effort.

As one course after another was served, Rose complimented each dish and savored them with such relish it reminded Will he ought to express his appreciation to Mrs. Wilder. He took her culinary skill for granted, when not many housekeepers could wear a cook's hat as well.

He considered Rose's impoverished childhood and wondered what meals she would have eaten—or done without. Her life had been so different from his privileged existence. In all his years of living in London, he had never ventured to Spitalfields. Perhaps a visit to view firsthand how the other half lived was overdue.

"Mr. Carmody, I understand you tutor university students," Rose said. "Do you enjoy it?"

"Yes, I do. I had thought at one time I might become a professor, but realized I would not feel comfortable facing a room full of students. Private lessons are easier."

"And better for those who are struggling. I understand lecture halls are often full to capacity and the pace is fast. I know I would need more time to absorb a new concept."

Will longed to know how Rose had gained the education she possessed, for working class girls scarcely attended school. Aside from occasional lapses, Rose's grammar and accent were impeccable—perhaps Hattie's influence. But he could not ask such a personal question.

"I was Carmody's first pupil," Guy joined in. "We met at uni, where I was more intent on having fun than putting my nose to the grindstone. Will coached me to sit for examinations."

"When you bothered to try, you were actually an excellent student."

"I'm afraid I formed a bad habit of lazing about then hurrying to catch up. But I am applying myself at last and succeeding quite well, don't you think, my dear?"

Hattie regarded him with pride. "Indeed. You've moved several members of Parliament toward the suffrage cause. Not an easy feat, given the disposition of those particular gentlemen."

"And I commend you for your support of small businesses. I could not have achieved my goal without your loan," Rose added.

Guy fanned himself with one hand. "Stop. Your compliments will swell my head until I'm unbearable."

"Too late. Modesty has never been your strong suit," Will automatically retorted, before realizing he and Hardy's usual banter might not be appropriate. The ladies might think him rude or jealous of his friend's accomplishments, which wasn't the case. Teasing was simply a part of their friendship. "In all seriousness, you have become so dedicated and responsible that I cannot help but admire your efforts. Well done, Hardy."

"Thank you." His friend's smile and the little duck of his head indicated how pleased he was to receive his praise. Guy's father had never shown an ounce of pride in his son, so Hardy was overdue for some commendation.

"How is our investment coming along by the way?" Guy asked Rose. "Your shop seems busy whenever I've stopped in, and it is only your first month open for business."

"I could not ask for better success. I'm nearly overwhelmed with customers. In fact, one day, when I had an order to fill, Mr. Carmody aided me by waiting on them, earning my undying gratitude." Her smile made Will want to serve her every day.

"You ought to hire help. Perhaps your sister?" Hattie suggested.

Rose avoided the question by asking one of her own. "How is Margaret catching on?"

While Hattie assessed the skills of her new assistant, Will pondered Rose's reaction concerning her sister. Was she estranged from her family? She'd mentioned feeling an outsider. Did they pester her for money? Did they even know of her success? More questions he dare not ask.

"Being the only women who own shops on Providence Street is sometimes a challenge," Hattie said. "The other merchants have become accustomed to the idea and occasionally accept our suggestions during association meetings, but we must sometimes endure subtle digs or innuendo."

"Not always so subtle," said Rose.

"Who? What do they say? Tell me who has been rude to you and I'll take care of it," Guy demanded.

Hattie smiled fondly. "That's very noble of you, my knight errant, but it is nothing I can't handle. Most of these slights you might not notice even if you were in the room. But a woman can detect a patronizing tone directed at her."

"And leering looks which they think pass unnoticed." Rose shook her head and stabbed her spoon into the lemon sorbet.

Shocked, Will reviewed every time he'd snuck a look at Rose. Had his gaze lingered long enough to make her feel uncomfortable? Perhaps he'd been leering rather than admiring. How was one to know the line between the two?

"Concerning the orangerie," Rose diverted the subject. "Mr. Carmody, have you ever traveled to a Mediterranean country and visited a grove?"

"I was once in Italy on holiday, but I was only intent on studying Roman ruins."

"Oh, what a marvel!" Rose clasped her hands. "I would enjoy going any place, as I've never been out of London. There is so much to see in this world."

"I'm afraid I've read about more places than I've actually visited. Perhaps it is time I considered visiting some of them." *With you as a traveling companion, exploring new sights.*

Guy talked about a trip to the Alps he'd once taken, then described the honeymoon tour he would like to take with Hattie.

"I don't see how I could take that much time away from the shop," she protested. "Don't forget I will continue to be a business owner as well as your wife."

Guy regarded her with a more solemn expression than Will had believed his friend capable of. "I would *never* expect you to forsake your career. It would be like asking you to stop breathing. I fully support your professional achievement. You do know that, don't you?"

Hattie paused long enough to suggest perhaps she had *not* been so certain of it. "Then how can you suggest we take a month long gallivant about the continent?"

"Margaret could live above the shop and manage it during your absence. You would remain in close contact with her via telegram. If anything dire should occur, we would cut our trip short and return." Guy showed he had considered the matter. "After we have settled into our home together I would certainly not expect you to become some sort of *hausfrau*. When we marry, your independence will not be in jeopardy, I promise."

Hattie sucked in her lower lip and frowned. "I imagine at some point we might have children, which would change everything."

"There are nannies," Guy replied.

"I wouldn't want my little ones raised by a stranger. I plan to spend time with them."

"As do I. And as a gentleman of means and leisure, I will have many hours to devote to our progeny."

"You, caring for children?"

"Since I am rather a child myself, I would be a wonderful playmate, and Nanny could help a bit with the looking after. I would bring the children to see you at work whenever you wish. You might hire a second assistant if you want more free days. Trust me, I've considered this from all angles. I will be the best sort of father, providing excellent attention and fun times for all. Discipline too," he added quickly.

Will stared at his melted sorbet. The discussion was almost too personal to witness.

But Hattie's abrupt snort of laughter made him look up.

"You *would* be!" she said warmly. "I can't imagine a more loving man to father a child, nor a more supportive husband. So, Mr. Hardy, if you are still willing to marry a quite stubborn and often distrustful woman, I would like to set a date for our wedding. What about late autumn? We could spend the cold winter months touring Greece and Italy. Would you marry me in fall?"

"I will!" Guy pronounced enthusiastically.

Will glanced at Rose, who grinned at him, clearly delighted by the unexpected turn in the conversation. She lifted her glass. "To the happy couple."

"Here, here!" Will agreed. "May you enjoy a long and joyous life together. To paraphrase Plato, a true union is that of disparate souls complementing each other, thus growing in compassion, affection and love."

As everyone drank the toast, Will wondered if he could ever find such a so-called "soul mate." Rose Gardener had made it clear she had no interest in him, yet he couldn't help his gaze returning to her during the avid discussion of wedding plans that followed.

AT THE END of the night, Miss Gardener assured him when next they met, she would have a plan to present. "We will design a room that will be a quiet retreat for you, a place of solitude and peace."

More solitude was the last thing he needed, and peace and quiet were quite overrated, Will thought as he saw his guests out the door. But at least he would have an ongoing reason to see Miss Gardener. Even if it was only for her friendship and gardening expertise, that would be worth everything.

CHAPTER EIGHT

ROSE STRIPPED THE stem of another larkspur as vivid a blue as the day's sky. She attached the delicate flower to a thin stave for support and plunged it into an array of larkspurs and hydrangea blossoms. Blue was what Lady Cromwell had requested, so blue she would get.

The repetitive motion gave her mind plenty of time to wander to her plans for Mr. Carmody's conservatory and to the man himself. Since the dinner party several days earlier, both had rarely been out of her thoughts.

Upon first entering his home, she'd been overawed by her surroundings. But talking with Carmody made her realize even high status did not prevent a person from feeling lonely sometimes. Rose found herself missing thoughtful, soft-spoken Mr. Carmody with his gentle ways. Now that he'd stopped making excuses to buy flowers, she would like to see his towering figure fill her doorway once more. But, since she'd disabused him of any romantic notions about her, that was not likely to happen.

Why, precisely, had she driven him off?

Her feelings toward him had shifted somewhere along the way. Thoughts of him now started a little wriggle in her stomach. But warring with that interest was the knowledge that nothing could come of any special friendship that might develop between them. So why start what could not come to any good end?

The shop bell summoned her from the work room and her thoughts. Because she was thinking of William Carmody, Rose somehow imagined the customer would be him. Her spirits rose.

Instead, she received a gut punch of shock. "Mum! What are you doing here?"

"What? Too good to greet yer old mum properly?"

"Of course I'm pleased to see you, but it is such a surprise. You haven't come to visit once since I opened the shop."

"Well, I'm 'ere now." Mum tucked back a hank of her hair, once as red as Rose's, now faded and streaked with gray. She glanced around. "Lots o' flowers. You sell this many in a day?"

"No. But I have to offer variety and appear well-stocked. It is what the customers expect." She felt a defensive need to explain herself. "One must expect to lose some stock. It's the nature of the business."

"Oh, must 'one,'" her mother mocked. "Whaddya do with the blooms at end o' day, toss 'em in the rubbish bin?"

"An old friend from the market picks 'em up. Remember Gram's friend Mary Pardo? She 'as a bit o' luck sellin' nosegays outside the opera house." Like shedding a layer of skin, Rose returned to the bones of her being, a Cockney lass aping her betters and pretending to belong in their world. "What can I do for ya, Mum? Why've you come?"

"Ain't you friendly tho'? Afraid one of yer fancy customers might see me?"

It was precisely that fear which made her dart glances at the door. "Of course not, Mum. I'm 'appy you finally came, but I expect you want somethin'?"

"There's a coal bill needs payin'." Her mother's gaze drilled through her like a sharp stave pinning a flower into place.

What sort of coal bill could there possibly be during a steaming hot summer? But Rose did not dispute the claim. "I can contribute a little to help with that."

"And yer sis is up the duff from one o' them Barnes boys."

"Arietta is pregnant?" Sadly, it was not a surprise. "Which Barnes? Sam or Job?"

"Naw, the other. The one who went for a soldier come 'ome for 'is dad's funeral and set his eye on our Arietty."

"Gus? But he's so old! He must be near forty and Arietta is only fifteen."

Mum clicked her tongue. "Almost sixteen, and so was I when I wed yer dad. What's yer point?"

"Are you sure she wants this?"

"Don't matter what she wants. It's done now, innit? Anyhow, the fella's a sergeant an' makes a good wage. 'E'll be takin' 'er to back to Inja. So there's Arietty sorted."

Her little sister swept away to a foreign land, likely never to be seen again. Though the two of them had nothing in common except blood, Rose prayed Arietta would be happy with her lot. "When is the wedding? I'd like to see her before her big day."

Mum wagged an arthritic finger. "Don't you be interferin', puttin' codswallop romantical notions in her 'ead. Tis for the best."

"What do Dale and Danny have to say about it? I expect they wanted to beat Gus's hide."

"'E offered to put a ring on 'er finger right away, which is right and proper. Yer brothers knew it and so did yer Da. You ought to be celebratin' too. Didn't you say you wanted the girl out o' the factory?"

There was no arguing that. But she should have asked her sister to work for her. She might have saved her from both frying pan and fire. Instead, she'd been more concerned with Arietta's rude manners. She hadn't wanted her coarse sister to deter clients. If she'd only guided and mentored Arietta as Hattie had done her, the girl might not be in this fix.

"Gus must return to 'is regiment. Took leave only long enough to put his Dad in the ground and find a good English girl to take back to that heathen land. If ya want to see yer sis, you'd best do it soon."

"I could come to supper tonight. Is there anything I can bring?"

"A ham would be nice, and a smoked mackerel as well?" Mum created a shopping list on the spot.

"Will Dale and his family be there?" Rose assessed the number of mouths she had to feed.

"I'll tell 'em to come by six."

"I can't make it that soon, Mum. I have to close the shop and buy the groceries. How about seven?"

"Whot about that coal bill then? Can ya spare a quid?"

Much more than a hod cost, but Rose gritted her teeth and retreated behind the counter to withdraw some money from the till.

Her mother crammed the bill into her dress pocket. "Yer a peach, Rosie."

"Sure." Rose knew most of the money would be pissed away on gin before reaching either the coal bin or the landlord. It was hard to break the habit of handing over her paycheck to her mother. Next time, she would insist on paying any bills directly.

"Ta then." Mum walked out of the store, leaving a gamey scent that nearly overpowered the flowers and a feeling of despair that made Rose's shoulders slump.

Exhaustion from holding her body so rigidly and biting back negative words overtook her. She despised herself for feeling embarrassed by her own kin, fearful that a customer might walk in and witness their encounter. That guilt, plus worry over her sister's fate, prompted tears.

Rose turned the sign to closed and retreated into the back room to cry in peace. She loved her parents, her brothers, her little sister, her flesh and blood and the bane of her existence. But she would never understand how they could be so content with their lot and so mean to each other.

Rose became aware of a rapping on the shop door. Some customer, undeterred by the sign, demanded her attention. Rose wiped her eyes and went to answer the relentless knocking.

But the woman on her doorstep had not come for flowers.

"Miss Sweet!" Rose noted Candace's harried expression, with eyes as red and swollen as hers felt. "Come in."

She put an arm around the dark-haired woman's shoulders to usher her inside, and locked the door behind her.

"I'm s-sorry," Candace whispered. "I did not know where to turn and needed so desperately to talk with someone, but I should not have come here."

"Nonsense. I invited you, remember? Let us sit in my kitchen. I will make tea while you tell me all your troubles."

ONCE SHE HAD Candace settled, Rose sat studying her friend's worried eyes. A demure dress, buttoned to the collar, covered her lush figure. She appeared as soft and vulnerable as a puppy one wanted to cherish and protect. What had her fiendish relative done to frighten her so thoroughly?

"Has your guardian bothered you again?" Rose prompted gently.

The woman dipped her chin. "I can hardly bear to put voice to it."

"Telling me might help you to unburden yourself."

Her guest paused, then nodded more firmly as if making up her mind. "It is not I who should be ashamed. It is he who continues to force his unwanted attention."

Rose's stomach dropped. She prayed that attention had not gone further than lewd comments or looks. She waited patiently for Candace to continue.

"As I mentioned, he has been looking at me in what feels like an inappropriate manner. This afternoon, prior to changing for dinner, I sat facing my vanity mirror and pondering my future. Suddenly, I realized I was not alone. My guardian had entered the room unannounced and stood watching me brush my hair.

"I put down the brush and tightened my dressing gown, under which I wore no more than a chemise and drawers. Mr. Merker moved behind me to rest his hands on my shoulders and study our reflection in the mirror. He said..." She swallowed and hugged her arms around herself.

"He complimented my physical endowments, expressing his admiration for ample-bodied girls. The words weren't as alarming as his gaze roving up and down my form as if I wore nothing at all."

Rose shivered, feeling the disturbing moment as if it were her own. "You poor dear. What a horrible creature."

"I felt I must remove myself from that room before something happened. But his hands weighed on my shoulders, keeping me in the chair. He told me his feelings for me had grown since my return from France. I was no longer the child he had cared for, but a young woman ripe and ready to entertain suitors. He pointed out that plump girls might not easily find a match, but I need not worry. I could remain in his home forever so far as he was concerned. He would always cherish me."

Candace drew a shaky breath. "I knew he was on the verge of proposing and would expect an immediate, joyful response. I also believed if I didn't give it, he would attempt to force me to accept. So I pushed back my chair back, knocking him off balance. I lunged up, excused myself, and fled from the room."

Rose's heart beat fast as she imagined running from that devil. "Did he come after you?"

"No. I hid in the water closet until I heard my maid's footsteps pass by. Then I returned to my room, dressed myself, and came directly here. I did not pause to pack or to plan. Now I have no idea what to do. If I return, I must play the dangerous game of putting him off while still living under his roof. I will not say yes to his proposal, of course. The idea of such a marriage is unthinkable. But if I refuse him, what might he do? Keep me locked up until I comply? Declare me mentally unfit and send me for treatment of some sort? Or worst of all, force himself on me in a physical manner? Possessing my fortune is probably the larger part of his keen interest, but I fear there is more to it than that."

"The bloody bastard wants to control you and have power over you, because it makes him randy," Rose declared.

Candace nearly smiled at her outburst. "I have not heard that expression, but I can guess its meaning and fear it is the case. I apologize for bringing my burdens to you. I suppose I must go back at some point to collect my things, but after that..."

"It does not seem safe for you to return home. Stay here until you have gathered your thoughts and decided what to do next. My rooms are upstairs. Please, pass the night, and feel free to wear my clothing."

"That would be too much to ask. I have a little money I've managed to save. Enough to rent a room, I hope, although I'm not really sure. As I said, my guardian has never trusted me with spending money, insisting on paying my bills for me."

"If you are to build a future without him, you are likely to need every penny of what you have. Stop the night here, and perhaps by morning your way forward will seem clearer."

"Really? Are you positive? I would be more grateful than you could ever know."

Rose stood. "No arguments. I'll show you where everything is."

She felt some trepidation as she showed the well-bred young lady around her simple flat. What had seemed homey to Rose now appeared well-used and cheap. But Candace exclaimed, "How charming! Your home is so cozy."

After making her guest comfortable, Rose realized the hour was growing late. "I'm sorry I must leave you for a bit. I must attend a family supper tonight. Please, make yourself at home. Eat anything you wish from the larder. I will return as quickly as I possibly can. I would not go at all, but there is a bit of a family emergency I must attend to."

Lovely almond shaped eyes widened. "Oh no! I hope it is not serious. How ungracious I've been, speaking at length about my worries and never asking you one thing about yourself. When you return, I promise to offer a listening ear."

Rose smiled. "I imagine by the time I'm through with my family I shall be too upset to do anything other than curse like a sailor. This is not likely to be a pleasant evening."

CHAPTER NINE

SHE HAD FORGOTTEN how crowded Mum and Dad's flat could be with the entire family there, along with extra relatives, friends, and neighbors shifting in and out. There'd never been a large enough table to accommodate them all. People perched where they could with a bowl full of the ham, which Rose had brought, and Mum's watery cabbage soup. Her mother had been quick to scold her for not bringing smoked mackerel as requested. *Eat last, in case there ain't enough to go around*, she advised.

At least the sponge cake Rose brought made her little niece and nephew cheer. Somebody showed gratitude for her effort.

Sweating bodies, bellowing voices, and lack of fresh air made the packed room a chaotic blur of noise and motion. Rose felt like a bit of flotsam floating on this rough sea. These were her people, yet she felt no more akin to them than strangers she might meet on the street. Her arrival was hardly noted since everyone was in the midst of an argument about who should pay for Arietta's wedding party.

"Barnes can afford it," Dad shouted. "Let him foot the bill. Least he can do since he got her up the duff."

"Gawd's sake, Dad! Don't be such a skinflint. It's me weddin' and you ought ta pay." Arietta's face was nearly as red as her hair. A little mound already showed beneath her dress, making Rose wonder exactly how long Gus Barnes's leave from the army had been. Long enough to have fathered this baby, or would he be raising someone else's child as his own?

"Arietta!" Rose shouted above the din. "Come outside so we can talk."

Though they hadn't seen each other in many months, her sister barely spared a glance. "Bugger off. I'm busy talkin' to Dad, the ole penny pincher."

"Please. It's important."

"Fancy gown that. Where'd you get it?" Madge, Rose's sister-in-law fingered her sleeve.

Mum came from the other room, bottle in hand. "Fancy, indeed. Showin' off her duds like a peacock. Why dontcha buy a weddin' dress for your sis. Think o' someone besides yerself for a change."

"Arietta. Come on! Move your bleedin' arse and maybe I *will* buy you a dress," Rose used the only language her sister understood.

A few moments later, the pair of them stood in the tenement hallway. It stunk of piss and sweat, but at least it was quiet enough to talk without yelling.

Arietta folded her arms over her full breasts. "Goin' to scold me for gettin' knocked up?"

Rose held her tongue. "What's done can't be undone. But I would like to talk to you about your future. Do you truly want to marry Gus Barnes and live in India? Once you go, you won't likely return, you know."

"Anyplace is better than 'ere. Ain't that what you used to say?"

"But that is not always true. What do you know about him? Is he kind? Will he treat you right?" She didn't ask if Arietta loved him for she felt fairly certain of the answer.

"'E's awright." Arietta shrugged. "Gus fancies me and wants to set me up in a proper 'ome. Says e's tired of bein' alone and don't want to look around no further for a wife."

"You don't have to marry yet. You're so young."

"Mary and Daisy and Carrie is all either wed or about to be," Arietta listed several of her friends. "I'm glad to be set and outta this hellhole. Could do worse than Gus, who's stickin' by me even though I'm—" She put a hand to her round abdomen.

"What if there was another way?" Rose hesitated. Could she take on the responsibility of her pregnant sister? She should want to, but it was hard to make the offer. "What if you came to live with me and worked in my shop?"

For a moment, as Rose looked into her sister's face, it was a mirror of her own, eyes bright blue and open rather than squinted in a perpetual frown. Arietta's mouth dropped open and she looked very young with her expression so unguarded. "You want *me* to come work for you?"

"I could not have you in the shop where your condition would raise questions, but I would teach you how to care for the flowers and make floral arrangements."

"Why the 'ell would I want to do that, you silly bint?" Arietta laughed. "I got a man set to look after me for life. I don't gotta work as no shop girl, just take care of me 'ouse. A real place of our own and not a flat, Gus says. I'm gonna live like a queen in Inja."

Rose hated how relieved those words made her. "You're really sure this is what you want?"

"I told you it is. Sheesh, get the wax outta yer ears."

"In that case, I'm happy for you and wish you the best of luck. Let me know if there's anything I can do to help with your wedding, like supply flowers."

"A fancy dress 'd be nice. Somethin' like what you got on, but a brighter color and shinier."

Rose glanced down at her simple day dress. "I can do that. What color would you like?"

"Pink," Arietta answered promptly.

"You always did love pink," Rose murmured. "Like your doll's dress."

"Yeah. Remember when Jamie Dawson took her from me and pulled off her arms? You beat him up proper."

"I did." Rose cuffed Arietta lightly. "No one could mess with my sis except me."

They smiled at one another. Then Arietta snapped, "So, you comin' inside or not?"

"Not tonight, but I'll see you again before your wedding so we can make sure the gown fits. Will that be all right?"

"Sure." Arietta glanced at the door from behind which raucous laughter exploded. "Don't blame ya. I wouldn't go back in there if I didn't 'ave to. You done good to get away and make somethin' of yerself. Don't let any of 'em tell ya otherwise."

"Thank you. I guess you've done well for yourself too, finding a good man to care for you." She hoped her words were true.

Rose watched Arietta disappear into the flat then walked down three flights of rickety stairs to the street. She hadn't bid anyone farewell, but guilt no longer stalked her. Her family was a world apart from her new life. Only relief rode with her as she headed toward the home she had built for herself.

ROSE ENTERED HER flat to find her distraught guest sleeping on a pallet of cushions and blankets on the floor. Candace's expression smoothed in slumber made her appear much younger, merely a girl like Arietta. The obvious solution to Candace's problem became instantly clear. The woman needed sanctuary and a way to earn money. Rose needed an assistant. The fit could not be better, if the genteel young lady were willing to work in a florist shop.

WILL SAT AT his usual position at the family dining table on Mother's left, across from Rupert and his wife Virginia. Penelope would normally sit beside Will, but his younger sister was off to the Alps with friends.

"Lady Smyth mentioned you haven't responded to her invitation. Surely you must have received it by now," Mother pressed.

"I have and will reply soon." Will changed the subject, "Rupert, how is your new horse?"

"Fine, fine. His sire was Lord Codsworth's Bright Legion, you know, and his dam a fine filly from Edgeworth stables. This foal should be a great jumper and fast as lightning. In fact, we've named him Lightning Bolt, haven't we, Ginnie?"

Virginia whinnied with laughter. "Indeed. Finest horseflesh as I've ever seen. You must come out to the stables after dinner to see him, Willie. He'll murder the steeplechase with that lineage."

"I should like to see him." It was easy to keep quiet after that and allow his brother and sister-in-law to fill the dinner conversation with talk of breeding stock. It seemed they took more interest in their racehorses than their children, Rupert Jr. and little Gerald.

The boys were, of course, up in the nursery. Will had spent the afternoon hour with them upon his arrival and found he enjoyed indulging their little whims. He joined in their game of soldiers, earning the title Uncle General from Rupert. It might be pleasant to have children one day, he had thought. Until Gerald hit Rupert in the head with a block, ending the session in howls and tears. Ginnie had separated them with aplomb and helped Nanny carry them off.

Will could not think of a better suited couple than his jovial brother and even-tempered sister-in-law. Like a perfectly matched pair of carriage horses, they moved in harmony, assured of their place on the earth and that paddocks filled with horses and a nursery filled with children were the epitome of happiness.

His gaze wandered to his father, who was silently consuming halibut. Will had inherited his quiet and solitary nature. Father ran the estate efficiently, steering it into the modern age with dexterity, and making certain all the tenants prospered. But when it came to managing the rest of his life, Mother was in charge, and he seemed happy to concede to her opinions. She might occasionally ask his opinion, then do precisely as she originally intended. But they seemed content in their symbiotic relationship.

Meanwhile, Penelope's role in the family was to aggravate, spend money, and get into tight spots, but always come out smelling like a rose. His outgoing, independent sister dubbed herself *a modern girl*, yet Will glimpsed very traditional traits under her surface. Mother predicted Penelope would soon quit her high-stepping ways, marry, and become a bastion of the London social scene.

This was his family. And who was Will? The sibling who was never quite up to snuff, always lagging a bit. He refused to marry, procreate, or perform stunningly in some field. Politics, Mother had suggested, even though he had never shown any inclination in that direction. She told Will he behaved like a hermit and it was high time he emerged from his cave. He supposed she was right. She usually was.

With Rupert and Virginia running full bore about Lightning Bolt's future prospects at Aintree, it was easy to sit meditatively chewing fish. Will exchanged a look with Father, who winked at him.

Abruptly Mother interrupted the horseflesh tutorial. "Speaking of bloodlines, William, I highly hope you will make yourself amenable to the young ladies at Lady Smyth's party."

"Mother, I have heard your wishes on the subject several times. Let us speak instead of the conservatory. The repairs are finished and I have hired a horticulturalist to advise me on the plantings."

"I'm so pleased to hear it, although you might have consulted with me. How many happy memories I have of that room. Now that you appear to have developed a fondness for plants, perhaps you might like to tour my gardens after supper."

"Certainly, so long as there is no further talk of Lady Smyth's party."

His mother held up her hand. "I promise. I am not one to belabor a point, you know."

WITH DINNER FINALLY finished, Rupert and Virginia walked to the stables with Father, while Mother took Will's arm to stroll through the brightly blooming rose garden. How his Rose would love her namesakes here, Will thought as he inhaled the sweet aroma.

Mother pointed out each variety, calling them by name. Then she abruptly stopped walking and her gaze remained fixed on a drooping cluster of pink Damasks. "Son, I would venture to bring up a delicate subject with you. I am loath to broach it, but—" she took a breath—"I feel it is time."

Will braced for a barrage about the many reasons to marry and sire children. "Mother, there is no need. I will attend the gala if it is that important to you. I will be nice to the young ladies and dance with them despite my two left feet."

She clicked her tongue impatiently. "Please, allow me to speak. This is not easy. What I wish to say is that I—your father and I—understand you may remain a confirmed bachelor all your life." She exhaled with a whoosh as if letting go of something she had held in for a long time.

"Yes, I am a bachelor and likely to remain so." He thought again of pretty Rose, who was not interested in him, and knew he spoke the truth.

"You mistake my meaning. I am talking about a specific *sort* of bachelor. Someone like your Uncle Leopold, if you take my meaning. If such is the case, I will stop driving you toward marital prospects and we will speak no more of the matter ever."

Will took a moment to for the gears to whirr and her meaning to click into place. His great uncle had a private secretary, a very nice chap who had served Leopold for many years. It was understood by the family, and probably most of society, that this companion was something more than an employee. The longevity of their bond suggested something much deeper.

"No! That is to say I am not *that* sort of confirmed bachelor." Will wanted to laugh and to cry at the touching thought that his parents had not only discussed his sexual preference, but also decided to accept him if he were of the queer bent.

"No, Mother," he continued more calmly. "I admire ladies quite a lot actually. I simply don't present myself well to them. We have little in common, the ones you introduce me to at any rate. If I were to choose a woman to wed merely to have a wife, it would not be fair to either of us. I long for someone with whom I might exchange ideas and conversation and laughter. When the right woman comes along, I will know it."

Rose could be all of those things, his heart chimed in.

His mother regarded him curiously. "You're holding out for some fairytale version of love."

For the first time, he wondered if the judgment he'd always felt implied in her tone had perhaps been in his own mind. "I suppose you could say so, but I don't see it that way."

"Very well, then." She nodded in a decided manner Will knew all too well. She'd worn the same look when commandeering Rupert and Virginia's wedding or when convincing the church congregation to donate more generously toward building repairs. This was his mother's expression when she got things accomplished.

"I shall continue to present potential candidates, while attempting not to be too overbearing," she promised. "I know of a bookish, very sweet spinster who has been on the shelf for a number of years. Perhaps she might suit."

"Perhaps." Will pulled her into a brief, fierce embrace. "Do you know you truly are a remarkable woman and mother?"

"I do. Your father often tells me so."

WHEN HIS FAMILIAL duties were finally over and he'd driven back to London, Will flopped onto his well-worn leather chair in his library haven.

He thought about Mother's amazing pronouncement, and he thought about his recent attachment that might have headed slowly toward the altar if it were given a chance to grow. The only woman who had ever claimed his interest upon first sight, making his soul cry *Her!* was Miss Rose Gardener. The trouble was he could not pursue her against her wishes. It would be tantamount to forcing himself upon her.

Yet shouldn't a man try to demonstrate his determined affections so a lady understood his commitment? There was no equation for this unsolvable math problem. He must simply live with it until the solution became apparent.

CHAPTER TEN

ROSE STOOD IN the center of Mr. Carmody's conservatory and took a slow turn. She had planned the appropriate measurements for the beds and plantings, but now wondered how her vision could fit in this modest space. At the end of her turn, her gaze came to rest on the room's owner.

Today, Carmody wore a shirt with sleeves rolled up, and no vest or jacket. In his casual attire and with his hair carelessly tousled, he seemed more boyish and approachable, not the grandly attired host from the other evening. She liked the suspenders striping his chest. An unaccountable urge to pull them out and let them snap back made her grin.

Carmody returned her smile, sunlight glinting off his glasses. Deep creases bracketed his mouth, drawing attention to nicely shaped lips. The man was breath-stealing when he smiled!

Her stomach did a little swirling dance like a chicken feather floating to land softly on the ground. Rose dropped her gaze to the copy of the blueprint in her hand.

Carmody moved close to study the plan over her shoulder. His body radiated heat that made her sweat—or perhaps that was due to the sun lancing through the glass panes. She thought she felt his breath caress her temple, although he was not standing *that* near. Prickling urges squiggled up and down her skin like ants, except not at all unpleasant.

She completely lost her train of thought as she attempted to point out features on the blueprint. "So you see…" She went mute, staring at the paper and trying to suppress her new feelings for Mr. Carmody.

Or were they new? They had begun to stir the night of the dinner party when his height, which at first she had likened to Frankenstein's monster, no longer seemed alarming but alluring. Rose had noticed the difference in his posture that night, no longer stooping but with an erect bearing that commanded attention. She liked this confident version of Carmody, who did not mumble or stammer when he spoke.

"I see what you've done here. Yes. The varying heights will make a stunning display, and a few large rocks placed among the ferns will give a natural effect." He reached around her to point out several spots as he spoke. A whiff of his scent, shaving cream and sweat, excited her senses. "I had not thought of a koi pond."

"I-I—" Now Rose stammered like a child who had not memorized her lessons. "I am glad you are able to overlook the crudeness of my sketching."

"You're a blue-ribbon artist compared with me." His low chuckle sent another army of ants scurrying up her spine. She should find a better comparison, for the sensation was more akin to flesh gliding against flesh. What would it feel like for his finger to trace a pattern on her back? For his wide palms to span her waist? For his lips to cover hers?

Rose coughed to cover her small whimper. "Have you a glass of water? It seems rather hot in here even though the windows are cranked open."

"Perhaps we did not choose the best day to meet. It may be the hottest day of the summer yet. I shall ask Reardon to bring iced lemonade."

Carmody stepped away from her and she felt the temperature recede. Rose followed him, trying not to study his rear as he led her from the conservatory into the library annex.

"Please sit. I am sorry I allowed you to become overheated without offering refreshments." He removed a pile of books from a chair facing a larger leather chair grooved by the shape of his body. Then he went to the electronic bell push to summon the butler.

Sitting stiffly on the edge of her seat, Rose imagined Carmody lounging in his throne of a chair, king of a bookish empire. Her gaze wandered across the books lining shelves, stacked on a table and even in piles on the floor. She read the titles of several near her: *The Philosophy of Money. The Case of Mr. George Edalji* by an author she recognized, Arthur Conan Doyle. *Enlightenment for a New Moral Age.* Out-of-place in this illustrious collection was a children's book: *Ozma of Oz* by Frank Baum.

Rose picked up the book and leafed through it, smiling in delight at the illustrations of Mr. Baum's magical world.

Carmody dropped into his chair. "You've discovered my secret weakness for children's fantasy stories. Some late nights when tomes on weighty topics are too dark, there is comfort in retreating into lighter fare. Carroll's Alice was a favorite in my youth. Recently, there has been a surge in children's literature, including works by Baum, E. Nesbit, Hodgson Burnett and the satirical *Cautionary Tales for Children* by Hilaire Belloc—definitely *not* intended for the very young."

Rose closed the book on a beautiful illustration of the fairy ruler of Oz and stroked the embossed cover. "How I would have enjoyed reading such fantasies as a child. I possessed only one dull moral epistle distributed by church missionaries, all about Pious Penelope and Naughty Nancy. Still, I read it until the binding fell apart. I coveted more interesting tales from the bookseller's cart but could not afford to buy anything, so I would hover nearby and when the vendor was busy, I'd read whatever I could get my hands on as quickly as I could. Eventually, he would notice me, slap my hands, and tell me to move on."

"Unforgiveable! No child should be denied books. I support an organization that distributes free reading materials to the needy, and children most especially. The plan is to someday establish lending libraries around the city in poorer neighborhoods."

"What a worthwhile endeavor," Rose exclaimed. Yet more layers to this kind man who gave his time to tutor students and his money to make certain everyone had books to read. His generosity warmed her.

"Please, feel free to borrow anything you like from my collection. Why don't you peruse the shelves now?"

Rose did not need more prompting to browse the library shelves. The books, both ancient and freshly printed, exhaled a delicious papery odor with every page she turned. She could have explored for days, reading snippets of this volume or that in Mr. Carmody's extensive library.

After Reardon arrived with their lemonade, she resumed her seat.

"What are you currently reading?" she asked, before sipping the tangy, iced drink.

"The horticulture book and an anthology of Sir Arthur Conan Doyle's mysteries. The latest is a case of a damsel in distress—aren't they always?—who beseeches Holmes to find her missing guardian whom she believes has absconded with her fortune."

Rose thought of Candace, except in her case it was the damsel who had disappeared—and without her fortune. Her guardian must have police searching for her by now. Would Merker eventually track her down and force her to return home?

"Mr. Carmody, could you recommend someone who might provide legal advice about inheritance and the age of majority?" Rose interrupted.

If he was startled at the abrupt question, he was too polite to show it. "No doubt my solicitor, Mr. Jennings, has knowledge of such matters."

"I'm asking for a friend, so I may not share details before consulting her," Rose explained. "With her permission, perhaps your solicitor might help with a very delicate situation."

"I should be happy to retain him on her behalf."

"Thank you. I would greatly appreciate it." She wanted to share her burdens with him, to confide about Miss Sweet, and also her worries about Arietta's future. Mr. Carmody was such a sympathetic listener. But neither topic was appropriate for discussion.

He had gathered a stack of children's books for her to take home, and now she studied the cover of a green volume with a gold embossed figure playing a flute. "*Peter Pan in Kensington Gardens,*" she read aloud. "Is this based on Mr. Barrie's play?"

"The opposite. The Pan character first appeared in Barrie's book *The Little White Bird,* then the stage play, and last year the author published this volume with charming illustrations by Arthur Rackham."

Rose leafed through the pages, examining the mischievous, magical illustrations. She had not been to the theater, but one couldn't live in London without having heard of this play written especially for children. "Would you read a chapter aloud, Mr. Carmody?" she asked impulsively.

"If you wish?" He took the book from her, opened the volume, and began to read, "*All children, except one, grow up…*"

Rose settled in her chair, took another sip of her beverage, and fell in love. The story of the boy who never grew up was poignant, but it was the reader who brought the tale to vivid life. With a book in his hands, any stiltedness disappeared. William Carmody portrayed the characters, his voice lightening to a tenor for Peter's and Wendy's voices, and dropping into his natural bass timbre as the narrator.

Rose drifted on the waves of his voice, as secure and content as if in a boat she knew could not possibly capsize. His cadence carried her along, weaving an enthralling spell. No adult in her recollection had ever told fairytales to her as a child. What a wonder to relax and be transported to a nursery somewhere in London, eavesdropping on a flying lesson that used happy thoughts as fuel. The impossible became possible, and Rose mentally cheered as Wendy and her brothers took to the air.

In addition to her childlike delight in the story, Rose felt the physical response of a mature woman listening to the sensual voice of a man. William's spectacles rested low on the bridge of his nose, his hazel eyes more brown than green in this light. The sharp angles of his face begged to be touched. She imagined the feeling of smoothly shaven skin stretched over hard bone underneath her exploring fingertips. She also imagined his deep voice murmuring endearments in her ear as his hands caressed her body.

Just as her fantasy grew too excruciating to bear, Carmody ended the chapter and closed the book.

"Oh no! You can't stop there," she exclaimed. "I want to see Neverland."

He took a long swallow of his lemonade, nearly emptying the glass. "You may read the rest for yourself."

"Not the same. I am enjoying your acting. You paint such a clear picture."

"Mr. Barrie's words."

"You have a lovely reading voice," Rose complimented. "When I visit again, perhaps you might read another chapter. But I suppose we ought to get to work now, making a list of supplies for the project."

"I've ordered soil which will be delivered soon. Now I must place orders for the plants from nurseries I've researched."

"But you've only just seen my plan. Are there no additions or changes you wish to make?"

"Miss Gardener, I have implicit faith in your vision, and I'm eager to begin."

"We needn't wait for builders to tear down the old planting tables. With those out of the way, it will be easier to envision our garden. I mean… *your* garden," she corrected.

"It is such rough labor. Your hands…"

"I have done hard work all my life. It does not bother me. So, shall we get to work?"

CHAPTER ELEVEN

FROM THE MOMENT Miss Gardener stepped into the conservatory, Will scarcely heard the details of her proposal. She glowed with animation and inspiring enthusiasm, and he desired her with a fierceness brand new to him. As she came to a conclusion, he nodded and offered an appropriate comment while corralling his wild longing in a secure paddock.

Once he'd gotten his feelings penned, he became a better listener, enjoying their talk about books and their importance to children. He would have read himself hoarse if Rose demanded it, but he was equally glad to put Pan's adventures aside and join her in tearing out the old planting tables.

Using a hammer, he applied brute force to knocking boards apart. Rose carried the pieces through the outer door to pile them behind the garden shed. When Will straightened to relieve pain in his lower back, he noticed Rose watching him with a curious expression. Was it admiration? No, he must be imagining her interest. Nevertheless, he posed a bit, drawing back the hammer to deliver a blow that made the wood crack.

"Let me have a go. Looks like fun."

He surrendered the hammer to her and watched with delight as she knocked out a table leg.

"Bloody 'ell but that feels good!" Rose immediately clapped a hand to her mouth. "I'm sorry, Mr. Carmody. That was rude."

"Do not apologize. I appreciate your enthusiasm. And, we are to be friends, might we address each other by our given names? Please call me Will."

She smiled as she passed him the hammer. "Then you must call me Rose...Will."

For a moment they both stood, grasping the handle of the tool, warm and a bit slippery from perspiration. When Rose looked at him, Will fell into the cool blue pools of her eyes.

"I—" Any thought he might have formed blew away. He could only lock gazes with this woman who with equal ease made delicate bouquets and wielded a hammer as if it were a weapon.

A sheen of sweat glistened on her forehead, her cheeks pink as a prize rose. Her magnetic gaze drew him closer until their faces were inches apart. He viewed her blurry face through the steam on his spectacles. Will shook himself from the trance. He had promised to maintain professional distance. He would never force his attentions on a woman or—

Rose pushed up onto her tiptoes and pressed her lips to his.

Will grunted in surprise and let go of the hammer at the same moment Rose did. It hit the floor with a *thunk* as they reached for one another.

Sliding one hand around her waist, he supported her head with the other so he might kiss her more deeply. Damp and soft as petals, her lips parted under the pressure of his mouth. *This* was kissing. How had he managed to reach thirty years old without experiencing an act that seemed as necessary and natural as breathing? Rose's quiet hum of pleasure assured him she enjoyed it too.

Any self-doubt or wavering vanished as instinct instructed him how to hold her and kiss her, and where to allow his hands to wander. He molded them over her hips, feeling her hipbones and waist through her light cotton day dress. Rose had flung her arms around his neck, grappling him close and pressing her body tight against his. His manhood thickened as it hardened. Surely, she must feel the bulge pressed against her skirts.

This might be a good time to pull away. You know where all these good feelings may lead.

But Will did not want to stop kissing and holding her. If he did, they might come to their senses and the glorious moments would be over. He *had* to have just a little more of this passion before reason resumed authority.

He gently sucked on Rose's lower lip then dared to caress the tip of her tongue with his. The sensation was pure bliss.

Rose pulled away only to breathe and gasp softly, "Oh!" before plunging back in for this deeper connection.

Heat built between them in the sweltering greenhouse, until it was difficult to tell how much was lust and how much was the intense afternoon sun. Will shuffled backward toward the door to the library, bringing Rose along with him.

He tripped over the hammer. Rose stumbled too and kept herself from falling by grasping Will tightly, a hand landing on his arse. He swept her off her feet like some rake in a gothic novel, and carried her through the doors into the library. Rose did not beg him to stop like a damsel in a story would have. Instead she looped arms around his neck and leaned into him, kicking the door further open as they passed through.

He tossed his misty spectacles toward the library table and placed Rose on a large ottoman, shoving aside books to make room. Unaccustomed to the day's activities, his back wrenched and pain radiated up his spine.

He groaned.

She let go of his neck, eyes wide. "Are you all right?"

"It's nothing." He knelt before her, face was level with hers. Rose regarded him with those lovely eyes, caressed his cheek, and touched his lips with her fingers. Blazes shot through Will's body from every point of contact. Back pain forgotten, he kissed her fingertips, then took her hand to kiss every knuckle and nuzzle the soft center of her palm.

"Ooh. That feels lovely," she whispered, offering her other hand.

Will knew instinctively how to touch her. He felt in his bones and blood precisely what she wanted, innate carnal knowledge percolating through him. He nipped the fluttering pulse in her wrist before moving up her inner arm with nibbling kisses that prompted soft sighs.

His hand came to rest on her thigh and he considered pushing up her skirt to find stockings, garters and feminine flesh. God, how he wanted to touch those things! But it was a border he would not cross. There must be some restraint to his passion. Instead, he massaged her leg through her skirts and that seemed to please her.

"Oh," she moaned. "Oh, Will! Just... just a little higher."

He moved his hand to where leg met torso, one finger venturing even higher. As he continued to massage, Rose groaned louder, then stopped kissing him to pant, "Oh...my...Gawd!"

Her body went stiff in his arms.

Will pulled back to view her parted lips and fluttering eyelids. Her blissful expression told him something had occurred, but there instinct failed him, for he wasn't quite certain what it was.

After a moment, Rose opened her eyes to look dazedly at him. "You... That was... I am so embarrassed."

"No! Have I offended or hurt you in some way? I apologize."

She reached for his hand, holding it to her chest beneath which her heart pounded. "You did nothing wrong. I enjoyed it. A bit too much. I shouldn't have come undone like that."

Will was still confused about how he'd brought her ecstasy with a simple touch. These were not things a man was taught. Even Guy had never spoken in detail about his experience with ladies.

Rose smoothed away his frown with a touch. "I never meant for things to become so overheated. Perhaps it prompted by our exertions in the conservatory. But you mustn't be concerned. I enjoyed it very much."

"I am glad. Even if my behavior was improper, kissing you is the best experience I have ever had. I would happily do it again."

"Maybe not just now," she said gently. "For I fear where further contact might lead."

As quickly as this storm had blown up, it was over. He had crossed a line, and she regretted their romantic interlude.

He shifted away. "I understand," he said, although he felt like howling in disappointment. "I will not bother you again."

"You misunderstand. I do not wish to end this aspect of our friendship. But for today we ought to take a moment to consider." She grasped his hand between both of hers. "I like you, Will Carmody, more than I anticipated. I said our friendship should remain uncomplicated, but my feelings have begun to change. Have yours?"

He peered into her face, a bit blurry without his spectacles. "My feelings have not altered since first we met. They have only grown with every encounter. The more I come to know you, the more assured I am that you are a lady of the finest caliber and I am the luckiest man alive that you would grace me with your presence."

Rose's lips parted on a slight gasp and then she smiled. She must think him an overly emotional dolt. He should have stuck to his habitual silence rather than spout poetic nonsense.

"Those are the most beautiful words anyone has ever said to me… William. But I cannot imagine what amazing qualities you believe I possess. I am not at all special."

"Ah, but you are, Miss Gardener. Your beauty is a given. But more than that, you are bright, industrious, independent and imaginative. You make grand plans and then work to execute them. I have witnessed what a stalwart friend you are to Hattie and to Guy. My admiration for you is legitimate, I assure you."

"You paint a perfect picture of me, but that is not all of who I am. I have quite a temper, and can be selfish and dogged in pursuit of something I want."

"Determined! I would add that to the list. What I cannot imagine is why you would have any interest in me. I am nothing to look at, nor am I charming like Hardy."

"Surface charm is not the best of qualities. I like that you don't make clever idle talk, although you have a dry wit on occasion. When you speak, I immediately trust what you say is true. And if I did not find your appearance appealing"—She swept her gaze slowly over Will's body, making him squirm—"You may be certain I would not have thrown myself at you today in such a madcap fashion."

She regarded him with a penetrating gaze. "In fact, I feel the desire rising again, so I believe I will take my leave, giving us both a chance to calm ourselves." She leaned forward and kissed his cheek chastely.

Will closed his eyes at the light touch and the brush of her breath as she spoke again. "May I see you again very soon?"

"Yes, please." He rose, took her hands and pulled her up to face him. Without thought or second guessing, he placed his arms around her as if they belonged there. "I understand your schedule is rather more hectic than mine. Whenever you would like, give me a call on the telephone. Will you please, Rose?"

A mischievous smile curved her lips. "I most certainly will."

CHAPTER TWELVE

"YOU ARE IN a fine mood this morning." Candace paused in her watering to regard her new employer. "What transformative magic has occurred to make you sing as you work?"

"Was I?" Even as she replied Rose could not control her grinning or the little song that repeated in her brain. It was a tune played on the carousel in the park across the street. Often the strains of the calliope drifted on the breeze to bring the whirling ponies directly into the shop. Her heart felt rather like one of those painted horses now, galloping in mad circles and getting nowhere.

"Maybe not singing, but you are humming. Might it have something to do with your appointment yesterday? Did you find Mr. Carmody's conservatory quite to your liking?"

Rose answered as if she was not aware of Candace's teasing tone. "I did. We removed some old tables and as soon as the garden beds are finished, we are very excited to begin planting."

"Mm-hm." Candace resumed watering.

Rose feigned a punch to her shoulder. "You are entirely too saucy for an assistant. I must say you too appear to be in a great humor today."

"Because for the first time in years I feel unfettered." She exhaled deeply. "Madame's school was as structured as any military unit, and since returning to London, I've done nothing but fear my future. I still have no idea what it holds, but thanks to your kindness, I am out from under Mr. Merker's roof. I cannot sufficiently express my gratitude for this freedom."

"Stuff and nonsense. You are doing *me* a favor. As you can tell after only a couple of days of working here, I desperately needed an assistant. You are a perfect flatmate as well, tidier than I am by far. We will get along wonderfully for so long as you choose to stay."

Candace's joy diminished. "But I cannot hide from my guardian forever. He no doubt has detectives or agents searching for me. There will come a day of reckoning, when I must stand against him."

"I hope you do not mind that I asked Mr. Carmody if his solicitor might help in the matter. Perhaps there is a loophole by which you might claim your inheritance early."

"On the contrary, I am greatly pleased!" Candace's skirt brushed against the freshly watered plants, dampening the dress she had borrowed from Rose. "I will appreciate any help as I have no idea what legal recourse is available to me."

"Then I will telephone Mr. Carmody to set a meeting."

"Can I trust his discretion? If word of my whereabouts got back to Mr. Merker, he might try to take me by force."

Rose took her hand and gave a supportive squeeze. "I'm certain you may trust William Carmody and his solicitor, but serving customers might bring unwanted attention. You should work with the flowers in back."

"I am of most use to you on the floor. No one in this city has seen me since I left for France five years ago, and rarely before that as I was merely a child. I doubt anyone would recognize my face."

"I fear for you, Candace, nearly as much as you fear for yourself. We should take precautions."

A customer swept into the store like a strong wind, interrupting their discussion.

Rose recognized Lady Anne Cromwell, Guy Hardy's former lover and one of the wealthiest widows in London. Her ladyship's patronage could make a restaurant, or a shop, instantly popular, as her support of Hattie's millinery had done.

"I simply *must* have that arrangement in the window. The design is exquisite," the patrician beauty proclaimed without preamble. "Have it delivered to this address."

The lad trailing behind her carrying packages hurried to present Rose with Lady Cromwell's card.

Rose did not usually sell the display bouquet, but she would not turn down this opportunity. "I will telephone the delivery service right away and have it sent over."

Her ladyship took a long look around the shop. "Very nice. I will be certain to recommend the place. Prospect Street is fast becoming my favorite shopping spot. *Tres chic* for a once drab neighborhood."

Rose recognized her ladyship's chapeau as one of Hattie's creations and wondered if the woman knew her favorite milliner and her ex-lover were soon to be married. Would that prompt her to end her patronage of the Prospect Street shops? That was a worry for another day and there was nothing to be done about it.

As quickly as she had entered, Lady Anne blew out of the shop, trailing the scent of gardenias behind her.

"Who was that?" Candace stared at the feathered hat bobbing down the street through the front window.

Rose explained the importance of their illustrious visitor without mentioning her ladyship's affair with Hardy. The young woman's ignorance of someone as well-known as Lady Anne Cromwell underscored how isolated she had been kept from London society. Merker had been intent on controlling Candace completely, but she had escaped her keeper. Still, she held on to her freedom by a tenuous and easily snapped thread.

The day's work passed slowly while Rose's mind carouseled in circles. She had arranged for Arietta to come that very evening to try on her dress, and felt unaccountably nervous that her sister would finally see the florist shop. Even more nerve-racking was the stallion riding front and center on her merry-go-round: Will Carmody.

Their encounter in the conservatory yesterday had left Rose both elated and shaken. She had certainly not intended any of it to happen, but the intimate atmosphere and Will's magnetic presence had drawn her into his arms like a honeybee to pollen. She wanted him with a powerful longing she'd never felt before. The only thing akin to it had been her desire to open a shop.

It wasn't as if she had no experience with lovemaking. She'd kissed lads in her neighborhood, and chaps she had two-stepped with at the dance hall. On a date at a movie house, one fellow had fervently mimicked the passion of the lovers on screen. But Rose had never been inspired to see any of these beaus a second time. She'd begun to believe that so-called "true love" was a myth—until she'd seen Hattie and Guy together.

And now there was Will to further illuminate this truth. Yesterday, she had felt a stirring of feelings she could not deny for a man whom she had once deemed awkward or snobbish. How wrong she had been. He contained so many facets—intellect, shyness, caring, trustworthiness, and gentle sweetness—that made him a diamond. He had always sparkled but she had been too blind to see it. Could she allow her heart to tumble willy-nilly into such powerful emotions?

She would only be hurt when reality put an end to the fairytale. The prince did not marry the pauper in real life.

When work was finished, Rose went to telephone Will as promised. Heart beating far too fast, she requested the exchange and the operator connected her. Reardon the butler answered, his stiff greeting making her even more nervous.

By the time Will came on the line, Rose felt like glass ready to shatter. Images and feelings from yesterday robbed her of reason, as she responded to his warm, "Hello! So good to hear from you!"

"Yes. Good hearing. To hear from you is good also," Rose mumbled. "I—wanted to ask… That is, I, um—" What had she wanted to ask him? She couldn't recall. Her heart pounded so hard she felt faint.

"How may I help you?" His resonate bass instantly prompted the recollection of him reading aloud to her. She wanted more of that sweetness, and the pulsing arousal his deep tone inspired.

She forced herself to breathe normally. "Do you recall I mentioned a friend in need of a solicitor? Her situation is quite grim."

"Oh." He paused. "Of course. I shall arrange a meeting with Jennings right away."

"That would be of great help to her. Thank you." She lowered her voice confidentially as if that would deter any person sharing the line from overhearing. "I also wanted to say how much I enjoyed our time together yesterday. It was rather wonderful, don't you think?"

"Yes! Very wonderful," he replied enthusiastically. "I had hoped I might see you again soon. Perhaps this evening I could take you to dinner."

"I would like nothing better, but my sister is coming to see me. She is to be wed soon and I've bought a gown for her."

"Congratulations to the bride. I pray she will find happiness in her marriage."

"As do I. She is very young and her husband decades older. They scarcely know each other," Rose confided. "He is stationed in India and will soon take her there with him. I fear I will not see her again in this lifetime."

The tears which made her throat ache every time she considered that, now rolled down her cheeks. The chasm between herself and Arietta would now be one of miles as well as opposing personalities.

"That is difficult. I am sorry," Will said softly. "But perhaps this man truly loves her despite the difference in age. Maybe he will cherish her."

His kind tone prompted more tears before Rose regained composure with a sniffle. "I apologize for weeping at you over the telephone."

"Please don't. I am happy you feel comfortable entrusting me with your feelings. If there is anything I may do to help, you must let me know."

"For now, I ask only that you arrange an appointment with your solicitor."

"Perhaps she might feel more comfortable talking with him at your place than at his office," Will suggested. "I will arrange something for tomorrow after the shop is closed."

"That would be perfect. Good night, Mr. ... Good night, Will."

After ending the call, Rose hugged herself and twirled amidst the ferns and flowers. She had a beau! Not the sort she had ever expected, but a kind and chivalrous gentleman. She wanted to sing out her news to the world, but must be content to hold the happiness bubbling inside her.

She went upstairs to inform Candace about the upcoming meeting to find the flat already filled with delicious cooking odors. Candace seemed determined to earn her keep by cleaning and cooking before Rose got to either task. The meals she made from simple ingredients were delicious.

But best of all were the sinfully delightful desserts concocted from chocolate so dark it was like black velvet on the tongue.

They had but a moment to discuss the solicitor before Arietta arrived direct from work in a patched dress with a few chicken feathers adorning the shoulders.

Rose introduced Candace as Violet, not knowing what her sister might do if there was a reward involved for news of the missing Sweet girl. Arietta managed the greeting politely enough before announcing, "I'm starved. Are we havin' supper?"

Candace assured them she had already eaten, then excused herself and went downstairs, allowing them time alone.

"How are you feeling?" Rose enquired. "Not queasy I hope."

Arietta patted the slight bulge of new life visible when her dress pressed against it. "Naw. Fit as a fiddle and 'ungry as 'ell. Mum says that's a sure sign of a boy."

"Sit then, and I'll—"

Before Rose could make the offer, Arietta already occupied a chair and had begun serving herself a bowl of stew.

Rose sat and watched her sister dig in, her own appetite subsiding. "Is your intended happy he might have a son?"

"Gus says this'll likely be our only kid as he's gettin' on in years. He don't mind that it's another chap's or that I ain't a virgin, which is 'ow I know he loves me," Arietta said. "What luck, eh?"

This was perhaps the most pitiful part of Arietta's thinking, the manner in which she assessed Gus as a worthy partner for her entire life. Rose wanted to enquire about the boy who had gotten her pregnant, but it seemed there was no point in it now. Instead, she asked, "How do you feel about Gus? Do you love him?"

"I like 'im well enough, an' that's better. We'll get on like people do, and I'll be livin' in comfort so…"

Arietta's pragmatism sounded exactly like Mum's, and Mum had made the mistake of marrying Raymond Gardener and falling in love with gin.

"You done right well for yourself, ain't ya?" Arietta took a look around the flat, Rose having already shown her the shop after letting her in. "Good for you, Rosie. Don't let Mum and Dad bleed you dry. You know they will if you let 'em. Already tried to get Gus to loan 'em money, the greedy blighters. And they won't pay a lick for my weddin'. Gus 'ad to cover that."

"Speaking of the wedding. Are you ready to try on the gown? I chose one with tucks at the waist to hide your condition."

Rose brought the dress out from her bedroom. Arietta gasped at the sight of the shiny pink satin dress, gaudier than Rose would have chosen, but she knew her sister's taste.

"Cor, I'll look like a bleedin' princess in that! And I can wear it at any parties the officers throw in Inja."

Did Arietta understand a sergeant was not on a par with commissioned officers? There would be no ballrooms in her future. Rose held her tongue.

As Arietta tried on the gown and Rose showed her how she might arrange her hair, it felt as if they were sisters in the truest sense of the word. The bickering and fisticuffs of their childhood belonged to Spitalfields. For the moment they might behave as friends without the pressure of living together in tight quarters.

After Arietta removed the dress and Rose placed it in a tissue-lined box, her sister asked, "What about you, Rosie? Do you never feature yourself wed to some chap? 'Ave you been romanced by many?"

Rose thought of William, but replied, "A few, but there's never been a lad I care about enough to marry."

"Aren't you afraid of bein' a spinster? You're already so old!"

"I'm only just twenty-two, hardly a crone." She refrained from pointing out that Arietta was too young to be wed, then found herself admitting, "Recently I've begun seeing a man who is..." How to describe Will in terms Arietta would understand. His intellect would not impress her. His money would. "He is kind, generous, and soft-spoken—all the things Dad and the boys are not. He would never yell or lift a hand in anger."

Arietta clicked her tongue dismissively. "What sort of man don't show some temper? Sounds like a limp-wristed dishrag."

Once again, Rose recalled why she and her sister had nothing in common. "He is not weak, and he treats me with the respect I deserve."

"Does 'e own a shop too? Can 'e set you up so you don't 'ave to work no more?"

"I *like* to work. I love managing my store. If you don't understand that, then you don't know me at all," Rose said crisply, then drew a breath. "I expect you had better get home now. I'll see you on your wedding day."

"Awright. Ta, then." Arietta held the dress box under one arm as Rose saw her to the door. Her sister left without a "thank you" for the gown.

Rose was not surprised.

Candace had been removing dead leaves and flower heads and now joined Rose. "Your sister seems nice. I always wished I had a sibling."

"You're welcome to mine." After only a few days, Rose already felt closer to Candace than to her actual sister. "I shouldn't complain. Soon enough she'll be gone, and I suppose I might miss her then."

"It is still early," Rose continued. "Would you care to meet my friend Hattie? We might walk over and see if she is at home. I promise you may trust her with your true identity, and she can be a great comfort."

CHAPTER THIRTEEN

"WHY DIDN'T YOU talk to me sooner? I'll get Rumsfield on the case and he'll find some solution." Guy paced Hattie's sitting room with his usual boundless energy, making it feel as if he were already getting things accomplished. "This fellow sounds like the very devil, so there's bound to be something to uncover about him."

"Detective Rumsfield *is* quite remarkable." Hattie offered a plate of biscuits to her guests and explained to Candace, "On our behalf, he learned the whereabouts of a missing young woman earlier this summer."

Candace regarded Guy Hardy nervously, clearly uncomfortable at meeting not only Harriet Glover but her fiancé as well. Guy had wheedled her story from her, and now was on a tear to resolve the situation.

"Rumsfield can dig up dirt on most anyone. You might be able to use what he finds in a court case." Guy barely paused in his pacing to snatch up a biscuit.

"Court case?" Candace repeated faintly. "I do not desire that sort of publicity. I simply wish to quietly earn my independence."

"Sometimes these things get messy. You may be in for a fight, so you should have all the facts." Guy spoke through a mouthful of biscuit, gestured emphatically, and scattered crumbs.

"Darling, you are not setting Miss Sweet at ease," Hattie pointed out gently. "This is her life. You've presented an option, now allow her the courtesy of considering it and making her own decision."

Guy swallowed, choked and seized a cup of tea. "You're right, of course. Pardon my overbearing nature, Miss Sweet. I often become too enthusiastic."

"Which is not always a bad thing," Hattie murmured.

Rose snorted with laughter, while Candace seemed oblivious of the double meaning.

"Well, you've got Will's solicitor anyway," Guy continued. "Perhaps you won't require more aid than that. I can't imagine why you did not call me right away. I have a solicitor too, you know," he scolded Rose.

"I didn't think of it. Mr. Carmody was uppermost in my mind." She hastily amended, "Because we have been working together in his conservatory."

"How is that project going, by the way?" Hattie's eyes asked a different question over the rim of her teacup.

"Quite well. We are nearly ready to begin bedding," Rose replied. "The plants! Bedding the plants."

Hattie pressed her lips tight to suppress a grin. "I'm certain you will both be happy with what you create together."

Rose glared at her while Candace and Guy weren't looking.

But Hattie seemed to be in an irrepressible mood tonight. "Mr. Carmody is a dear soul. If anyone may be counted on for support and faithfulness, it is he. I believe he has great depths one must deeply plunge into in order to fully know him."

Guy paused in his pacing to stare at his beloved. "What on earth are you talking about? We are discussing solicitors, not Carmody."

"Yes, darling. Of course." Hattie changed the subject. "Miss Sweet, do you have everything you require since you left home with nothing but the clothes on your back? I sympathize with your situation, my dear, as I long ago left my aunt and uncle with very little but my pride.

Would you care to view my wardrobe and see if there are any gowns you might use?"

"I fear nothing of yours would fit me." Candace regarded Hattie's thin form. "But I thank you deeply for the offer and admire your courage in changing your life. If it were not for Miss Gardener's friendship, I would not have been brave enough to flee."

Hattie touched Candace's hand. "Perhaps another day we might speak at length. I know it is difficult to discuss such personal matters with others present." She nodded toward Guy.

His eyes widened. "Oh! I am interrupting lady time. I am sorry. Shall I go home and leave you to it?"

"It is rather late now and I have much to think about. Thank you for your kindness, Mr. Hardy and Mrs. Glover." Candace politely ended their meeting. "You are great allies to have on one's side."

"Anything we may do to help, Miss Sweet. You are not alone," Hardy pronounced.

"Indeed," Hattie nodded. "You have friends now."

"PROFESSOR, I STILL don't understand. Please, explain it again." While Jasper Harkins had been floundering through algorithms, Will's mind had drifted into daydreams of Rose.

With a sigh, he drew himself back to the session and explained the particular formula for a third time. He had been tutoring long enough to know when a student simply wasn't equipped for a particular subject. Harkins and quadratic equations would never get on together. The young man was more interested in stagecraft, which naturally his parents were not pleased about.

"All right. I understand that, and that." Harkins pointed to sections of the problem. He pushed back his long bangs, the current mode for university students, which happened to make Will's always floppy hair suddenly stylish. "But what about *that*?" he stabbed his finger.

Will bit back his frustration. "Sometimes, Harkins, it is best to put aside a lesson when one grows too frustrated. Shall we rehearse your lines?"

"Yes, please!" The youth slammed his textbook shut, pushed his papers aside and offered Will a copy of *A Midsummer Night's Dream*. "I'm on pins and needles about my upcoming performance."

Harkins dove into Shakespeare's dialogue like a happy fish returned to a river. He played Demetrius rebuking his once-beloved Helena. Will took the part of the scorned maiden. He did not need to prompt his acting partner since Harkins knew every line of both parts.

When they'd finished the scene, Harkins sighed. "Why couldn't life actually be a stage and all people actors like Shakespeare says? Acting is all I care about, but my father has other plans for me."

"It often seems as if our roles are dictated to us," William agreed. "But you must get your marks, graduate, and then think about setting your own course."

"An actor doesn't need this sort of education. I should seize the day while I am still young. You are a lucky man to have the freedom to do exactly as you wish and love whomever you care to."

The last part was out of the blue, but struck a chord, since all Will could think about was Rose and what she might be doing at any given moment. "Are you enamored then, Harkins?"

The youth rested his head on folded arms and sighed again. "I am, but I don't wish to talk about it. Ours is a secret adoration. What about you, sir? You seem to have a new aura about you, and a look in your eyes as if your mind were miles away. Is there someone?"

"Not a suitable conversation for pupil and teacher, Mr. Harkins." Will found himself wanting to proclaim his feelings about Rose. The novel sensation of being in love was too heady to keep to oneself.

Harkins sat up, eyes aglow. "Inconceivable! A fellow of your age has found romance at last."

"Quite a presumption."

"Yet I am right, aren't I, and why not? Summer is the perfect season for it. Perhaps a private assignation in the woods just like in the play."

Rose *would* enjoy a spot full of natural beauty. He could whisk her away from the odorous city to enjoy some fresh country air. A vision of picnicking by a stream dissolved into a fantasy of moonlit woods and a grove blessed by fairies. A perfect setting for passion, as Harkins had said.

"Enough. Let us review your lesson once more then end the session. I have other tasks awaiting me."

With a groan, Harkins faced his eraser-smudged papers once more. Will led him through the process and by the end of a quarter hour his pupil seemed to have a marginally better grasp of the equation. After that, Will nearly shoved the chap out the door in his hurry to ready himself to meet with Rose that evening.

Hours passed with aching slowness as Will supervised the builders putting beds in the conservatory and cared for some plants delivered too early from the nursery. Tea passed his lips untasted, and at last he counted down the final minutes until Jennings arrived. The tall, thin man could have easily passed for a stereotypical undertaker from a Dickens story. His bony face and sunken eyes suggested mourning even though he was actually a genial fellow.

At the rear door of the florist's, Rose greeted them with a smile and an intoxicating whiff of perfume. Or perhaps it was merely the flowers she worked with, Will thought, as she ushered them up the stairs to her flat.

Inside, a doe-eyed brunette stood holding a plate of truffles, the chocolate sort rather than the earthy fungi considered such a delicacy. Rose ushered her forward and introductions were made.

Mr. Jennings' eyes widened at Miss Candace Sweet's name. "The missing heiress. Good heavens! Notice of your disappearance has been in the papers."

"We saw no word mentioned," Rose said.

"Then you haven't read today's *Times*. The article included an illustration, although I must say the picture does not reflect Miss Sweet's current appearance."

"Several years ago, I sat for a photograph to include in a Christmas greeting to my guardian. I was somewhat heavier then." Miss Sweet rubbed her forehead. "So Mr. Merker is publicly searching for me. How did the article explain the circumstances?"

"It did not hint at foul play, but suggested you had experienced a nervous interlude prior to your disappearance. Let us sit, Miss Sweet, and you may tell me your story," Jennings said calmly. "I do not take what your guardian suggests at face value."

Will would have greatly liked to learn more, but this interview should remain between solicitor and client. He excused himself, saying he would wait downstairs.

"I'll come with you. Unless you wish me to stay, Candace."

Miss Sweet shook her head. "No, thank you."

As Rose passed Will to lead the way from the room, the hairs on his arm rose like antenna, vibrating at her presence.

Once they reached the workroom and sat at the table, Rose filled him in on Miss Sweet's story. "Her parents died when she was young, leaving her to the care of a family friend. Now she is approaching twenty-one and he wants to wed her before he loses control of her fortune. She might protest, refuse him, and fight, but the law can make things difficult for a woman determined to gain her freedom. It is easier to believe her guardian has her best interests at heart, and heaven knows the lengths he might go to make her comply."

Will shook his head. "Horrifying! It is a disgusting scheme to be perpetrated by one who is meant to treat her as if she were his own child."

Rose drummed her fingers on the worktable hard enough to drill holes through it. "The law may find Miss Sweet of unsound mind and put her back into the hands of her persecutor."

"Rest assured, if there is some loophole in the law to be found, Jennings is the man to discover and apply it." Will attempted to sound reassuring, but the bleakness of the situation was formidable. It made him realize what freedoms he expected as his right, and how others in society were not so fortunate.

He covered Rose's madly tapping fingers so they stilled. "If Miss Sweet's guardian finds her and tries to coerce her, I promise *I* will not stand by and allow it to happen."

She regarded him solemnly. "Somehow I believe it. You are the most honorable man I believe I've ever met."

The shining intensity in her eyes nearly burned him. Will lowered his gaze as he asked the question he had determined to put forth before the evening was through. "This matter is so dire that I hesitate to ask what I am about to. I had hoped to invite you to the country this Sunday. I thought it would be lovely to get away from the city's heat. There is a stream at the edge of which we might picnic. Naturally, Miss Sweet is welcome to come with us."

"That sounds heavenly, and since I've never been out of London it would be a grand adventure for me. It might help poor Miss Sweet get her mind off her troubles for a bit. I would love to go."

Will bathed in her pure joy and enthusiasm. Having Miss Sweet as an additional guest may not have been his original plan, but he would gladly host both young ladies for an afternoon of leisure.

"Excellent! I will let Mother know we'll be out this weekend. She will have Cook make up such a picnic it will be a struggle to carry the basket."

Her smile froze. "We'll be picnicking on your parents' land. I hadn't considered that. But how will you explain our acquaintance?"

"I have no need to explain anything to anyone," he informed her blithely. But mentally he added, *Mother had better not dare question it or, for once, she will not find me such an agreeable son.*

CHAPTER FOURTEEN

ROSE BIT INTO another of Candace's truffles, the bittersweet chocolate charged with sugar melting on her tongue. It was her second, no, third treat that day, but she kept compulsively eating as she waited for Will to pick her up in his motorcar.

An automobile ride—the first in a day of firsts as she would be leaving London's foul air behind for a country interlude *and* meeting nobility as well. Her beau's parents were Lord and Lady Carmody of Carmody Hall, for God's sake.

"Are you certain you won't come, Candace? I will be without a chaperone."

"You'll certainly enjoy the day more if you're alone with your gentleman." Candace nudged the plate of chocolates out of Rose's reach. "And his family cannot be so very terrifying."

"But you'll have nothing other than worrisome thoughts to keep you company all day. What if…" Rose trailed off. She refused to plant the idea that one of Mr. Merker's agents might be watching the place, awaiting the perfect opportunity to take her away without a fuss. The chances of that were slight.

"Don't you worry about me. Have a last tidy up, so you're ready to enjoy your day," Candace insisted.

Rose did as she was told, primping in front of the mirror until she'd gotten her Gibson roll even and the curls at her temples artistically placed. At the roar of an approaching automobile, she fastened her traveling hat with pins and tied the gauze in a bow beneath her chin.

"An automobile ride. Imagine! It will be like flying," she exclaimed to Candace before she left.

"Have a wonderful day," her friend encouraged.

Rose hurried downstairs to meet Will before he even knocked at the door. He made a handsome figure in a long tan duster that swept the tops of his boots. Goggles were pushed up onto his riding cap although he still wore spectacles. A scarf wound jauntily around his neck completed the picture of a motorist ready to roar down the open road.

"What a pretty ensemble," he complimented her, his gaze saying more than words as he scanned her white dress and wide-brimmed hat. "But you should put this on lest you ruin your gown."

He held out a duster similar to his own while Rose slipped her arms into the long sleeves. Then he offered his gloved hand to help her onto the running board. She took a breath and placed her shoe on the metal step that vibrated beneath her foot. The purring engine hummed into her very bones as she slid across the leather seat. Every inch of this finely crafted automobile bespoke wealth from the gleaming chrome to the tooled details of the dashboard and the luxurious seats. It was far beyond any motorized conveyance Rose had ridden in before.

Rose sat back, hands clasped in her lap, as Will put the auto into gear and sped away from Prospect Street. The noise on the busy thoroughfare made it impossible to carry on a conversation, but soon they were beyond the city and passing neighborhoods then farms. The world she'd always known disappeared in the blink of an eye. She drank in the view of fields and meadows dotted with sheep or cows peacefully grazing, and she felt herself a mere speck hurtling along the road.

"Like a dab in a painting," she said.

"Pardon?" Will spoke above the engine's roar.

"Those paintings in the impressionist style at the museum. Little dots of color that require the viewer to step back to see the whole image. The world is very large and each of us a speck upon it."

"But all living things of importance, I believe."

"How should I address your parents," she asked abruptly. "Your lord and ladyship? Lord and Lady Carmody? Shall I curtsy? Perhaps we may take our picnic and not come across your family."

"I doubt that. I must stop for Cook's basket and take a moment to speak with Mother since she is expecting us. She will want to meet you and may show you her roses, something that will be of interest to you, no doubt."

What did his invitation today mean? What would his mother make of her son squiring a shop girl? How deeply would she glower? Dread eclipsed the bright sun of her excitement for the outing.

"William, when I agreed to go with you, I did not know it would be on your family property. I don't belong there and can't imagine your family will be pleased."

He removed one hand from the steering column and patted her clenched hands. "Do not worry. My mother should be happy I am accompanied by a female friend. She had begun to despair that I would ever bring a young lady to visit."

Rose stared at him. "I am the *first*? Do you not see how much worse that is? She will imagine I am of some import to you and that I am an opportunist stealing your affections."

"You *are* of import to me, and Mother would never view you as an opportunist." But his expression shifted slightly, suggesting he might have overestimated Lady Carmody's goodwill. "Everything will be fine, you'll see. As soon as I've introduced you, we'll take our lunch and set off to the stream."

Couldn't we skip to the second part? Rose wanted to beg. But she would not belabor the point. She must put on her best manners and behave the way she guessed one ought to in such august company. Still, she could not stop wondering why William Carmody seemed determined for her to meet his parents.

WHEN THE CAR passed through open gates between columns of granite, Rose's pulse drummed in a rapid tattoo. The automobile followed a curving gravel drive without a rut or a bump to mar its course, then rounded a bend where Carmody Hall stood in all its glory. Now Rose's heart nearly choked her. Blimey! The place was not a country house, but a bleedin' castle with turrets and crenelated walls. A princess might be standing up there fluttering a hanky. She would not be surprised to see a fire-breathing dragon rise up from behind the sprawling stone building.

"You never said," she accused Will.

"Never said what?"

"How grand it is. I could not have imagined this." The place was too much. The people inside would be far too grand for the likes of her and she'd make a fool of herself. She wanted to ask Will to turn the automobile around and head right back to the city. "I don't know what to say or how to act."

"Behave just as you normally do, and my family will find you as loveable as I do." Will's reassurance did little to put her at ease.

He drew up in front of the portico and hurried around to help Rose from the auto. She shook dust from the folds of the coat and pulled back the veiling of her hat so she might better view the stunning reflecting pool in the middle of the lawn.

Several servants erupted on the scene; a chauffeur claimed the keys from Will and drove the car around back to service it, and a butler welcomed them.

"Good afternoon, Mr. Carmody. I did not know the precise time of your arrival or I would have had the staff ready to greet you."

"Truly, Albertson, there is no reason to make a to-do. This is but a casual visit."

"I shall seat you in the drawing room and inform Lady Carmody of your presence. May I enquire as to your guest's name."

"Yes. Of course. This is Miss Rose Gardener. Albertson, our family butler."

Rose held out her hand. "Pleased to meet you."

Albertson stared at it before nodding curtly. "Miss Gardener." He led the way inside and to the drawing room before disappearing through the door.

"I've stepped in it, haven't I?" Rose asked Will. "It ain't…It's not correct to shake hands with servants."

"Not generally. But don't worry." He placed his hands on her shoulders and looked into her eyes. "It does not concern me if you don't follow the so-called rules to the letter. Please, sit down while we await my mother."

She smiled at him because she could not help but do so when he looked at her with those concerned eyes, but inside the words *await my mother* chimed a death knell. There was no bloody way the woman would view Rose with anything other than contempt.

As Will removed his spectacles and wiped away the dust of their journey, Rose examined the elegant room that could have held her family's entire flat inside it. Family portraits from past generations decorated the damask covered walls. The heavy wood furniture was well polished but underneath that gloss a patina of great age bespoke hundreds of years standing in those precise spots. Had Lord Carmody received his baronetcy from William the Conqueror? How far back did the Carmody lineage extend? She wished she had looked up the family in Debrett's peerage.

"Good afternoon." A cool, cultured voice interrupted the moment.

Rose stood to face a short woman with a ruddy complexion and eyes as intent as her son's. Rose dropped a curtsy she'd been practicing. "Lady Carmody, I am ever so pleased to meet you."

"No need for such formality." The woman glided into the room, her carriage erect and her stance patrician. Yet Rose noted the cuffs Lady Carmody's simple day dress were stained with soil as if she had come in directly from the garden.

"Mother, this is my guest, Miss Rose Gardener. I thought I might introduce her to you before we set out on our picnic."

Her ladyship nodded. "Good afternoon, Miss Gardener. Welcome to Carmody Hall."

Rose's knees refused to unlock so she might straighten from her curtsy. William silently took her elbow and helped her up. "I understand you raise prize-winning roses. I would greatly love to see them if it is not too much trouble," Rose blurted, since she could think of absolutely nothing else she might have in common with this woman.

Lady Carmody shot a glance at her son as if to ask *who or what have you brought home with you*, but she replied graciously. "Certainly. I am always pleased to show my *Lucinda Mays*."

Rose nodded vigorously and felt her hair slipping from its pins. She reached to steady her hat. "Might I freshen up, please?"

"Of course," Will said. "I apologize for not suggesting it right away."

Before he could summon the butler, Albertson appeared as if he'd been hovering in the hallway. He directed Rose down a corridor to a powder room.

Once inside, Rose collapsed against the door until she had brought her heart rate under control. She faced her reflection in the mirror. "You are meant to be a proper young lady, for heaven's sake. Don't behave like a bloody nincompoop!"

With her coiffure refreshed and her composure somewhat regained, she returned to the drawing room to find Will and his mother discussing some social event.

"You should ask Lady Smyth's permission if you wish to attend with a guest," Lady Carmody was saying.

"I will notify her soon. I promise."

At the sight of Rose, Will stood and directed her to a seat. Rose had hoped they might skip from uncomfortable conversation to walking in the rose garden. At least there, she and Lady Carmody might find some common ground.

"My son tells me you are a good friend of Guy Hardy."

"Yes, that's true. He invested in my floral business." No point in pretending to be anything better than she was.

"Ah, you own a shop," her ladyship said, as if that explained much. "William told me he had hired someone to help plan the conservatory. I am most anxious to see what plants you've chosen."

"Early days yet," Will said. "We have yet to begin planting, but I will hold a grand unveiling when we are finished."

Rose made an attempt to break free from the drawing room prison. "I had hoped to gain some inspiration from viewing your beautiful gardens here. Would you give a tour?"

"On the condition that you stay for dinner," Lady Carmody countered. "The rest of the family is hither and yon just now. I'm certain William would like for them all to meet you."

"That would get us back to the city far too late," Will said firmly. "Miss Gardener has but one day off. She must be at work in the morning."

"Yes, of course. I did not consider the rigors of being in trade. Perhaps another time." Lady Carmody stood. "Come then. While Cook readies your picnic, we will take a brief stroll."

Rose nearly sighed in relief as she fell in step with William, following behind his mother. She was not quite certain what to make of her ladyship, who on the surface seemed to accept her son bringing home a flower girl. But the comment about "being in trade" suggested her civil demeanor masked contempt and displeasure.

Annoyance at William for putting her in this situation bubbled up, but just as quickly quelled when he offered his arm and leaned to whisper, "Well done. We're nearly free."

Once Rose stopped fretting and took a look at her surroundings she nearly forgot her concerns. The Carmody gardens were breathtaking with terraced steps led from one area to another. As they passed through, Rose noticed some gardens were manicured to orderly perfection, while others flourished in a more natural state. She recognized many of the plants from the horticulture book, but there were varieties with which she was unfamiliar.

"What is that vine with the white flowers?" She pointed out the one in question to Lady Carmody.

Will's mother offered a litany of vines, groundcover, and ivies that lasted until they reached the rose garden by a circuitous path. "I'm afraid you've missed the very best blooms. This heat has brought the season to an early close."

The many species of bushes and climbing roses hanging over arches made this floral bower to delight a gardener's heart. "This is paradise," Rose exclaimed. "I've never seen anything like it. Not even in a park."

"Thank you, my dear. My gardening staff does the physical labor, but I spend time pruning as well. Heirloom varieties are my special passion, particularly as hybrids are now favored over them. I do not wish the old styles to fade away and be forgotten. History and lineage matter."

This comment seemed aimed directly at Rose. Inside, she shrank to the size of a Japanese beetle burrowing into one chewed blossom.

Lady Carmody noticed the intruding insect, plucked it from the petals and crushed it underfoot. "They're a menace." If she meant any personal attack by her words, it was not obvious as she now pointed out a bush of white roses with bright pink edging. "Here is what is left of my *Lucinda Mays*. They are mostly blown now, but there a few still blooming."

Rose inhaled the flowers' strong scent without needing to bend over. "They are exquisite and have a delightful aroma."

"Thank you. I'm quite proud of them if I do say so myself. The variety was awarded an Award of Garden Merit designation by the Royal Horticultural Society."

"How do you create a hybrid, your ladyship?"

Once Lady Carmody launched on the subject, Rose did not need to speak again, which made easy work of the slow stroll back to the house. The woman's enthusiasm reminded Rose of Gram's delight in flowers and any bit of nature she encountered on the busy city streets. That kinship, slight as it might be, put Rose somewhat at ease. Maybe she *could* fit into this grand lady's world and be accepted as part of her son's life—if their budding friendship came to that.

She glanced at Will, who had remained mostly quiet during their walk. The sun reflecting on his spectacles hid his eyes, but he smiled sweetly at her and gave a little nod of encouragement. In that one pure and perfect moment, Rose felt a surge of affection and entertained the thought that she might be in love. That was both a grand and horrifying idea.

"I suppose Cook has our luncheon prepared," Will interrupted his mother's discourse on aphid control. "Must be off before the day wanes."

Lady Carmody included Rose in a sincere smile that warmed her through. "I do wish you might dine with us, but I understand you must be on your way."

After returning to the house and bidding good day to her ladyship, they set off with a basket that weighed down Will's arm.

"I hope the meeting was not too uncomfortable for you," he said when they were some distance from the Hall. "I did not think it through when I suggested coming here, or I might have chosen some other location."

Rose did not take his words as regret for introducing her to his mum, but rather a desire to be alone with her. "So long as it wasn't the swamp in the woods Hattie told me," she teased, referring to a bog where Hardy had taken Hattie on Will's recommendation.

"It was a beautiful pond when I went there as a lad. How was I to know it had become so overgrown?" he protested.

They laughed together and Rose grasped the handle of the basket to share its weight as they strolled.

"Today's site will be much nicer, I promise. There is a lovely stream that cuts across the northern edge of our property. A bit of a hike, but there should be no muck or swarms of insects to ruin our enjoyment."

Rose very quickly realized she was not wearing appropriate shoes for walking over rough terrain. Her toes and her ankles ached, but it was worth the discomfort for the sight of a herd of cows with calves in a meadow.

"Look at the tiny one wobble! He must be a newborn," she exclaimed. "I must admit I have never seen living cattle before, only beef on a plate. I doubt I shall ever be able to consume meat again after this."

He smiled. "When I was a boy, I adopted a chicken that followed me whenever I was outdoors. I knew I could never eat such a faithful pet. But when Cook prepared him with apricot glaze, I devoured every bite. I should introduce you to her. The woman taught me practicality and how to make a loaf of bread from scratch."

Rose tried to picture young William sitting on a stool in the kitchen, chatting with the staff. How odd it must have been to mature from such familiarity to the proper distance between master and servant; polite yet removed. And where might an outsider such as herself fit in such a hierarchy?

Nowhere. It was not a world for the likes of her.

Her glum thought passed as they reached the stream. Its surface sparkled like diamonds in the sunlight, then flowed into the dim and dappling shade of trees. This was every bit a babbling brook such as those featured in books. Rose had never quite visualized the reality, having only gutters of rainwater to compare it to.

She dropped to her knees beside the swiftly moving water, scooped up cool water with both hands, and splashed it on her face.

"Don't drink," Will advised. "Cattle drink here and one cannot be too certain what they leave behind. It is all right to wade, however. My brother, sister and I splashed around here as children."

Rose sat back on her heels and looked up at him. "Tell me more about your siblings."

"Rupert and his wife Virginia live in the Hall with Mother and Father. They have improved the stables and are breeding racing stock. My nephews, Rupert and Peter, may be around somewhere as they are on summer holiday. They will return to school soon. And Penelope is touring Europe with friends. She is a bold spirit. 'A modern' she calls herself. You will probably take to her when you meet her."

The offhand way he assumed she would return and someday eventually meet his sister startled Rose. This budding romance was advancing far too quickly given all the obstacles to it. Although Lady Carmody had been polite enough, Rose did not truly believe the woman expected her to come to dinner. It was simply a polite invitation. Will's world could never be hers and it troubled her that he did not seem to realize it.

But no need to indulge in worry now while the sun shone and the brook babbled.

She watched the water pass by for several moments longer then went to where Will had spread a cloth and unpacked their luncheon.

Rose sank to the ground and loosened her shoes. She would like to shed them and plunge her sore feet into soft grass, but it would be inappropriate.

"Please serve yourself whatever you would like. Cook has packed sufficiently to feed an army; ham sandwiches, cold kidney pie, boiled eggs, pickled beets and her mouth-watering lemon-custard squares." He poured two glasses of wine.

Rose didn't wait to be asked twice as she attacked the bounty. She couldn't recall ever being so ravenous, not even the winter her entire family had been out of work due to factory closures and ill health. Back then, she had adjusted to meager rations. But now, having a veritable banquet laid out before her roused her appetite like an animal coming out of hibernation.

Will told about his childhood days playing in the stream with his siblings. "Our nanny was a lenient caretaker and let us run quite wild. Those were happy, carefree times, catching minnows, building forts, or playing at being highwaymen."

"There was a fort on our street, but the big boys ran it and the littles weren't allowed to join in. I played hopscotch and jumped rope with my friends." Rose avoided mention of her days as a button girl in a sewing factory.

In the comfortable silence following the meal, Rose savored the wine sending warm tendrils through her body. "This tastes like liquid sunlight."

"I'm happy you enjoy it. Would you care to walk alongside the stream, or wade in it?"

Rose paused for a moment, caught between decorum and having fun. "I would like that. I must confess my shoes are quite uncomfortable."

She quickly shed them, and Will did the same before rolling up his trouser legs. In this private grove, there was no need to worry about propriety and they might behave like children. Will took Rose's hand to pull her up and continued to hold it as they entered the water together.

The chill quickly numbed Rose's feet all the way to the ankles. She held her skirts high to avoid wetting them. Will's glance lingered on her legs, making them feel as hot as her feet were cold.

Stones poked here soles as they waded over the pebbles to a slower part of the stream. In that quiet eddy, fish made their beds on a smooth mud bottom. Rose watched in fascination as they fanned the dirt with their tails until they'd made perfect circles in which to lay eggs.

Will let go of her hand, rolled up his sleeves and joined her in her nature study. Crouched with forearms on thighs, spectacles in danger of slipping off his nose into the stream, and hair tumbling across his forehead, he appeared very young and playful. How had she once imagined him staid and stuffy? It went to show that most people had hidden depths society often forbade them to show.

"Aren't they a marvel," he exclaimed. "One forgets the wonders of nature when surrounded by city streets for too long."

"Have you decided whether to add a koi pond to your conservatory? It is not too late to include one in your plan," Rose said.

He regarded her, his eyes keen and bright above the lenses. "If you would like one, then I would too, for I pray you will spend time there once the work is finished."

Naturally, she enjoyed his appreciation, but once again it seemed too sudden for him to feature her in his future. "Why do you like me so much? Surely there are women who would better suit you, those of your own class."

"No. There are not. The debutantes my mother has forced upon me seem little interested in anything outside the social whirl. Their eyes glaze over when I mention any topic of interest to me. But you possess such intelligence and express interest in many subjects. I am completely content in your company."

He stood, towering over her like one of the trees that sheltered them. "From the moment I entered your shop and met you, I was smitten—with your appearance, naturally, but even more by your bright and energetic nature. Although at first I expressed myself with excruciating awkwardness, I have since grown at ease in your presence. I enjoy your friendship very much, and pray you feel the same way about me."

"I do." She waded nearer so she might take his hands. "I like spending time with you. But when you speak of future association that includes your family, I do not see how that will be possible. I am an interloper in your world."

He engulfed her hands in his. "You are *not*! And if any person in my family makes you feel so, I would end my association with them before I would end my friendship with you."

Before she knew what was happening, he swept her up into his arms and carried her to the bank. Throwing her arms around his neck, she snuggled close to his chest—enough to feel his heart beating. He laid her down on the cloth where they'd eaten lunch, breathing hard from his exertions and from something that made his eyes grow heavy-lidded and hungry. An answering flare of interest shot through Rose. They were evenly matched in a craving for something other than lunch on that blanket.

Keep yer legs crossed if ya know what's good for ya. Mum reminded her. Rose did not wish to end up in Arietta's predicament, but she could enjoy herself within reason.

Will knelt over her, his face coming nearer until her eyes closed in anticipation of a kiss. Doubts evaporated and Rose felt nothing but the sensation of his lips moving against hers. She opened to soft exploring warmth, the tip of her tongue meeting his. Electricity crackled through her and her body demanded *more!* as she wrapped her arms around him.

Through the cloth, sticks and stones poked her back, reminding her of the physical world. *Only so far and no further*, she recalled, but a stretching and opening inside her made her thighs tremble. She gasped for air, then plunged into deeper kissing, running her hands down Will's back to feel the warm muscle beneath his shirt.

Above them, birds chirped. Across heated flesh, a breeze blew.

Nearby, water splashed along its rocky course. But at this center of this, two bodies twined together discovering continents within each other.

Will cupped her breast through her dress and his clothed erection rubbed the throbbing point between her legs. She threaded her fingers through his hair and cradled his head, guiding his mouth to her breast, which had somehow shifted above her bodice's neckline. More lightning crackled where his lips, tongue, then teeth teased at her nipple. Rose's helpless moan prompted Will's answering groan.

He switched his attention from one breast to the other.

"Lovely! It feels so…" Her eyelids flickered open and she gazed the branches swaying overhead, sunlight peeking between them to dazzle her. Just like when he had touched her in the conservatory, the spot he rubbed against erupted and bliss washed through her. Rose closed her eyes against the sunlight and soared. "Oh!"

Will growled his approval of her response and after several more thrusts, he too froze. She understood the ecstasy which had overtaken her had also caught him up in its wild talons. An odd sense of pride filled her that she could bring him to that state. How wonderful for two people to move all barriers and become that naked—so to speak—with one another. Rose had never trusted a man enough to let him touch her so deeply, and not just in a physical way.

Was this what Hattie felt with Guy? Was this love?

The moment of bliss ebbed as Will moved to lie beside her. "I apologize," he murmured. "To invite you to this place and then take advantage. Please, forgive me. I did not intend to go so far."

Rose stopped him with a finger over his lips. "Don't ruin it with an apology. We both chose this, and I enjoyed it. Didn't you?"

"Of course! But a gentleman is supposed keep his baser urges in check and respect a lady." His hazel eyes appeared nearly as green as the leaves today as he gazed at her. "I want you to understand in what high esteem I hold you. What we did was marvelous, but I would not wish you to think it was my sole intent in bringing you here."

"I don't," she assured him. "Now stop fretting and let us enjoy the rest of our time together." She patted the blanket and Will reclined beside her once more. "Thank you for bringing me here today. This spot is lovely."

"Not as lovely as you," he replied.

"Now *that* is precisely the right thing to say."

He pulled her into his arms, and for several minutes they listened to the sounds of nature around them.

"I meant to tell you that Mr. Jennings is on the case, and I have also spoken with Hardy's Detective Rumsfield. Between them, they should be able to find a way to protect Miss Sweet from her guardian."

"It is criminal she can't simply to go to the authorities to help her," Rose replied. "She might try, of course, but he'd declare her mentally weak and they'd buy it. At least Merker never hit her. That's the way men keep their women in line where I come from."

Will's body stiffened. "Have you ever been hit by a man, Rose?"

"Smacks are a given where I come from. I've taken a few blows and handed some out as well." She snorted. "Anyhow, it's more honest than declaring someone loony to get your way. You must think us an uncivilized lot."

"Such treatment may hide under a veneer of gentility. Good breeding certainly does not eradicate violence." He paused. "I should like to meet your family. Maybe I could attend your sister's wedding with you if it is not too presumptuous of me to ask."

And there it was—the sledgehammer blow to her heart that startled Rose awake and knocked off her rose-colored glasses. Mr. William Carmody meeting the flotsam and jetsam of Cory Street? Inconceivable! She could never, would never take him there with her. The reality of the truth she'd been avoiding came home to roost like an ugly vulture in a dovecote.

Rose wriggled away from his embrace and sat up. "I, um, ought to be going. We've lingered too long and Candace might need something from me."

Will sat too. "I am sorry. I should not have asked. Please don't take offense, Rose."

She shook her head as she hurriedly gathered picnic things and shoved them in the basket. "I am not offended. But honestly, I cannot invite you to Arietta's wedding. And I think it best if, after today, we put some distance between us. There is much to consider. We both should take time to do that."

She said "consider" but actually meant "break it off." Her fledgling feelings for Will Carmody must end, for his sake as well as for hers. Hearts would be broken if they danced further down this garden path, and a stubbed toe of loss would be a great deal better than a gaping wound later.

CHAPTER FIFTEEN

FROM THE MOMENT Rose expressed her awed shock at the grandeur of Carmody Hall, William knew he'd made an error in bringing her there. He should not have introduced his mother on their first outing. Who was foolish enough to do that? Although, for several minutes in the garden, it seemed his gambit had worked. Mother seemed to like Rose. The differences in their station were forgotten as they discussed flowers. Will had laid some groundwork for the future. For he already knew, if Rose Gardener would have him, he wanted to marry her one day.

Their picnic by the stream, and what came after, reassured him he was on the right course. But then he'd gone too far by mentioning meeting Rose's family and the sun extinguished. She withdrew from his arms, declaring it time to go home.

As they shook out the wrinkled cloth and folded it neatly, Will realized "take time to consider" actually meant "let's remain friends." She was gently letting him know she did not wish to see him again. Not privately at any rate. He supposed they could not avoid each other at Guy and Hattie's wedding.

Feeling their golden moments slipping away, he attempted to bridge the gap. "Rose, I know I've pushed too far too fast, introducing you to my mother and asking to meet yours. This is the first time we've gone out together. I have frightened you with my intensity.

Please give me another chance."

She exhaled a long breath and stared at the stream. "I don't... I don't believe it is a good idea, William. I am attempting to apply some common sense. I know in my heart there could be no future we might share. Please, let us not fool ourselves about that."

"But there *is* hope of a future, if we are willing to try for it," he protested. "Please do not give up so easily."

Rose continued to regard the water as if she saw her entire life flowing by upon its surface. "I—I fear you are being unrealistic. Your family is grand. Mine is not merely a few pegs down the social ladder. We are below the bottom rung. You and I simply do not fit into one another's worlds, and there is no arguing with that."

He reached out to touch her arm. "Rose. Please, do not rush to a decision. You are part of a new movement that believes in equality. Should that not apply to social status as well as gender?"

When she turned to look up at him, he saw in her eyes her decision was already made. "You make a good point, but we do not yet live in that world. I believe we may remain friends, but that is all."

He could tell there was no point in arguing further. Not at this moment, at any rate. Perhaps, given time, she would reconsider.

"If this is to be the end of our romance, might I kiss you once more before we leave?" he asked.

She bit her lip before nodding.

Will cupped her cheek, so smooth and warm, and bent to press his mouth to hers. Her lips were as soft as the petals of her namesake. He lingered, savoring her taste and the slight puff of her breath against his upper lip. A breeze swept through the trees, making the branches tremble and the leaves rustle.

The melancholy feeling of life passing by swept through him like the wind. He could not hold onto one second of time, or to this woman, any more than he could stop the wind. Soon enough, Rose would shy away from even friendship, and Will would have only a memory of having once experienced love.

They did not speak on the walk back to the house, or on the trip to the city. Will stared at the road ahead, any words he would say would only repeat what had already been uttered.

Seeming lost in thought, Rose watched the passing scenery. Will wondered how was it possible to go from lovemaking to this distressing distance in less than an hour?

As he stopped the auto in front of Rose's shop, a mounting sense of dread filled him.

She looked at the dashboard rather than directly at him. "I had a lovely time, William. It was a perfect summer afternoon, and I will always cherish our private moments together. But truly it will be for the best to end our growing affection before our hearts become too involved."

Too late.

"To place some distance between us, I think it best you finish the conservatory project without my help. I believe it would be too difficult to remain friends only. Do you understand my reservations?"

"I do," he replied. *And they mean nothing to me. I would marry you this instant if I believed you would say yes.*

He would make that bold declaration if he believed she would agree, but Rose had made her wishes clear. Not so long ago, Will had counseled Guy to slow his pursuit of Hattie, respecting her decision and giving her an opportunity to perhaps change her mind. How facile that advice had been! It was a great deal harder to follow.

Pressuring Rose would be selfish now when she had clearly told him what she wanted. He had to bite his lip to keep from blurting his feelings and desire.

"I am truly sorry for encouraging you in ways I shouldn't have," Rose continued. "Hurting you was never my intention." She turned away, but not before he saw tears glistening in her eyes.

Before Will could come around to open her door, Rose was outside the vehicle, across the pavement, and entering her shop.

He watched her with dull despair. *Things were going so well. What happened?* his heart demanded.

But he had no answer to give it.

ONE COULD WALLOW in bed and while away days in mourning with the drapes drawn. Or one could get up, throw open the window, inhale a draught of fresh air and try to accomplish something. Will brooded for most of the following day before electing to follow the better course. After all, Rose had not entirely cut him from her life. He must learn to be content with her friendship. He'd prove his resolve by continuing to aide her with the Sweet matter.

Detective Rumsfeld had left a message while Will was out the previous day and apparently already had news to share. Will arranged an appointment by telephone then headed toward the man's office with purpose. One could not fight an enemy without knowing all about him. It was paramount to learn as much as possible concerning Edward Merker and his connection to the Sweet family. Why had there been no relatives to take her in? And how had he gained custody of their daughter?

Rumsfield's secretary ushered Will into the detective's messy, shabby office. Will hoped the chap's mind was more organized than his workspace. But Hardy swore by him, so Will settled onto a lumpy chair and waited to learn what the old man with the bulldog demeanor had uncovered.

Rumsfield sat puffing on a cigar and glaring at some paperwork. He removed the stub from between his teeth, dispensed with a polite greeting and cut straight to the point. "Don't know what the young woman's told you about her history. Her father, Sir Phillip Sweet, was minor gentry and the last of his line. No relatives to cluck about it when he married an Italian woman, Carlotta D'Arenzo. I couldn't learn anything about her family. He brought her to England, the couple married and had a child. When their daughter was eight, Sir Phillip and his wife both died within days of each other from a severe bout of diphtheria. Sweet's will left both fortune and daughter to his business administrator Edward Merker."

"An employee. Had the couple no close friends better suited to raising a child?" Will shooed away a wisp of smoke that stung his eyes.

"Perhaps Merker was the closest friend Sweet had," Rumsfield pointed out. "The arrangement was unusual, but the will appeared to be in order and the child properly looked after."

"So that's it, then? He will continue to control her and her inheritance until she comes of age."

"There may be grounds to question the validity of the will. Seems convenient the man had access to all of his employer's documents, property deeds, bank accounts, etc., and plenty of opportunity to practice his signature."

"You believe the will may have been forged."

"Wouldn't doubt it, but probably can't prove it. The fellow apparently increased her holdings and met Miss Sweet's needs—education and so on. Won't be easy to knock down a fellow like that in court."

"Even if he is attempting to force his ward into marrying him? Her protest against the arrangement should be enough to earn the interest of the law."

"Law isn't much interested in what a girl says," Rumsfield replied bluntly. "If she's found, she'll be returned to Merker's custody and he'll likely browbeat her into doing his will. Best thing would be for Miss Sweet to disappear until she's reached majority then claim what's hers."

"Meanwhile, he'll find a way to divert her money so she can't get at it. She'll be left with nothing," Will mused. "Why wouldn't the man have done that sooner if all he wanted was wealth?"

Rumsfield tamped out his cigar, which had filled the room with a smoky haze. "My guess, he wants to claim *her* as well. I've dealt with this sort in my line of work. They like the control and sense of power over a person. He wants the game to go on. If he gets his hands on her, he'll keep them around her throat for the rest of her life or as long as he's able."

"Then he must be stopped at all costs!" Will bolted up, too outraged to remain seated. "With these details, I shall have Jennings draft a lawsuit on her behalf as soon as possible."

Rumsfield nodded curtly. "Anything else I can help you with?"

"No. Thank you for your swift work, sir. Hardy was correct in his assessment of your skill."

The grizzled detective accepted the compliment as his due, sending William on his way with a simple "Good day" before returning his attention to other work.

Will left the office with Miss Sweet's situation uppermost in his mind, and only a portion still dwelling on Rose. He couldn't help but think of her since it was directly to her place of business that he went.

As he entered the busy shop, Rose was serving one customer, while her assistant wrapped a funeral arrangement at the register. Will grabbed a pot of African violets and headed toward her.

Miss Sweet's eyes widened at the sight of him. "Mr. Carmody!"

When her customer had walked away, he lowered his voice to speak. "Miss Sweet, I have news to share. Perhaps we might speak privately?"

"I hate to leave Miss Gardener with so many customers."

Will glanced around. "There are too many eyes that might observe. It may be unsafe for you here."

Rose joined them and immediately his body began to hum. That would not do, particularly if she noted his reaction. Will schooled his expression to politeness and nothing more. "I spoke with Rumsfield, who feels Merker may have forged the will, and that Miss Sweet is in a dangerous position. He suggests she go into hiding while Jennings presses a suit against the villain."

Miss Sweet frowned. "I've already decided I cannot remain here on Miss Gardener's good graces if I am of no use to her."

"Never mind that," Rose said. "It is more important you remain safe. We have been far too cavalier placing you in the public eye."

"Might I suggest my house? It is large, with several unused guest rooms. Miss Sweet would be safe there. My staff would remain discreet, I promise. I will have a room prepared for tonight."

"I scarcely know what to—" Miss Sweet fell silent as a customer bearing a pot of golden mums approached.

"This topic is better discussed in private. Shall I wait in back?" Will murmured.

Rose shook her head. "Miss Sweet and I will talk over the matter and telephone you. Meanwhile, go forward as you have planned."

Will nodded. He met Rose's gaze at last and the wall of reserve he had constructed began to crumble. How could he see her without his heart falling into pieces? Remaining friends would be a nearly insurmountable task for him.

But perhaps not for her. Rose's expression held gratitude and nothing more.

And so, as much as he wanted to pull her into the privacy of the work room and kiss her senseless, he could and would maintain a steady platonic course.

Friends. Comrades. Chums, he reminded himself as he exited the shop and set off about his business of championing Miss Sweet's cause.

CHAPTER SIXTEEN

"I AM NOT at all certain this is necessary." Candace fastened the valise Rose had lent her which contained several ready-made dresses she had bought since Rose's gowns were too tight on her. "Mr. Carmody seems very kind, but I do not know him at all and stopping at his house is inappropriate. It could cause great damage to my case, suggesting I lack moral sense."

Rose had her own doubts about this course of action, but would not tell the already nervous Candace. She rested her hands on her friend's shoulders and gave her a steadying look. "I believe Mr. Carmody is trustworthy. You may have already been spotted here due to our carelessness. You will be better protected with him while the solicitor lodges your complaint."

Candace bit her lower lip and traced the faded flower pattern on the valise. "I am afraid," she admitted. "It was difficult enough to come to you, a stranger, for aid. I can never thank you enough for inviting me into your home and making my troubles your own."

"If you are utterly set against it, you may stay, of course," Rose offered. "I have enjoyed your company and would not wish you to feel as if you have no choice in the matter. You absolutely do. As for bringing trouble, what are friends for if not to share each other's burdens?"

"I wish I could continue to help you in the back. There are all those arrangements for the Women's Parliament to prepare soon. Too much work for you alone." Candace drew a breath. "But Mr. Hardy is right about my drawing attention here. I imagine policemen coming for me in the middle of a work day. Such a scandal might ruin your shop, so I will go."

Rose would have assured her that a scandal was the last thing on her mind, but she did not wish to sway Candace's mind in the opposite direction. Will's home would be a much better shelter. His wealth and privilege could go far in keeping Candace safe.

The sound of a motorcar stopping on the street below announced Will had arrived to retrieve Candace. The two women hurried downstairs to meet him.

Rose gave her friend a comforting embrace. "All will be well." Then she went to open the door, heart beating far too quickly. She couldn't fool herself into thinking it was due to the drama of Candace leaving. Her anxiety had everything to do with seeing Will again.

When he'd come to the shop today, she'd managed to suppress any emotion, but it wasn't easy. The sight of Will standing there at the counter had drawn her like a magnet. The worst part was that she *knew* he would take her back. All she had to do was tell him so and they could be together. Doing what she felt was right for both of them was hard! She wished she could forget about their impossible future and seize the moment.

But Gram had taught her that putting off bills for another day would only make a person miserable and poor. Gram was where Rose had learned good business sense, and the woman's wisdom had not steered her wrong so far.

With a sigh, she assembled her face into neutral politeness and opened the door to Will's knock.

Two men in dark suits, the bills of their caps shading their faces, stood in the shadows of the alley. Freezing water coursed through her veins at the sight of them.

"Miss Rose Gardener?" the taller one asked.

"I am." At least she sounded calm even if her heart was beating an exit from her chest.

"You have a guest staying with you. Miss Candace Sweet."

"I have never heard the name before. I have no visitors here." She drew a breath. "If you'll excuse me, gentlemen, I was about to go out and you are blocking my way."

They crowded closer, one of them inserting a booted foot in the door so she couldn't slam it shut.

"Cut the malarkey, Miss Gardener." The second man might not tower over Rose like his partner, but his heavyset body and pugnacious stance suggested a boxer. He was short, tough, and loud. "A Good Samaritan spotted the girl and told the authorities. That's us. We saw her today. You're lucky we didn't make a scene in front of your customers. Now it's time for us to take the girl home."

"You're the authorities? Do you represent Scotland Yard? Have the police sent you? Please show me some form of identification." Rose listened for any sound from behind her, and prayed Candace had made her way upstairs to hide.

"Mr. Merker hired *us* to find his ward," the tall man said. "That's about enough of your questions, Miss. Let us do our duty."

The stocky fellow pushed Rose out of their way, slamming her body against the open door. He pinned her there, while his partner entered the room.

The agent approached Candace, who stood near the worktable with the valise clutched in her fist. "Now, Miss Sweet, no need to worry. We're here to take you home." He held his hands open to show he bore no weapon. "Come along now. Your dear uncle is waiting for you."

"He's not my uncle, and I will *not* come with you," she snapped.

As the man reached out for her, Candace swung the heavy valise so it hit his chest and kept him at bay.

Rose fought to free herself from the boxer's hand holding her pressed against the door. She could not pry his fingers from just below her throat, but her legs were free. She brought up one knee sharply into his privates. The fellow gave a howl and let go of her to reach for his groin.

Bent over, his head was right at the height of her elbow. Rose jabbed him hard with the point of her elbow and ran across the room to aide Candace. On the way, she snatched up the first thing in her path she might possibly use as a weapon—a bucket of flowers.

She heaved its contents toward the man reaching for her friend. A shower of cold water and cattails rained down on him. That slowed him down enough for Candace to slip away if she would.

"Run, Candace!" Rose yelled. "Go now!"

But the woman would not leave her. Instead, she bashed the tall agent a second time with her valise. The strength of her blow on his head drove him to his knees.

"Trenton!" The man bellowed. "Grab her."

His partner rallied from the shot to his genitals and did as he was bid. He seized Candace from behind, pinning her arms to her sides so she couldn't fit.

As he dragged her toward the open door, his partner scrambled up and faced Rose.

Before she could dart past him to aide Candace, he grabbed her arm with bruising force. Rose tried to scratch his face with her free hand but he was too tall. She screeched and bit at him, then kicked up with her knee but could made no contact this time.

"Don't make me hurt you. This is not your business," he growled as he restrained her arms by binding her body close to his. "The girl's going back where she belongs. If you know what's best for you, you'll let her go or face charges of kidnapping."

At his words, Candace immediately stopped struggling against her captor. "Leave Miss Gardener out of it. I was never kidnapped. She merely sheltered me when I came to her for help."

"Then you're gonna want to make things easy for your friend, ain't ya?" The short man took advantage of her stillness to remove a cloth from his pocket and clap it over her mouth and nose. Candace began to fight again, but he held her tight.

Rose watched as her friend's wide eyes above the handkerchief became unfocused, then closed. Candace's body went limp and she sagged against the fellow. Chloroform.

Rose renewed her struggle against the man who held her. She pushed so hard to break free that when he let her go, she pitched forward and fell on the floor. The tall agent gave a sharp kick to her ribs to make certain she stayed there.

For a moment, Rose lost consciousness of anything but the sharp pain in her side and the whoosh of air driven from her lungs.

When she looked up, the tall agent had lifted Candace's unconscious body as if it weighed nothing and slung it over his shoulder.

His partner stalked over to Rose. "This is for me bollocks, ya filthy twat."

The last thing Rose recalled was the toe of a boot coming toward her face.

WHEN SHE AWOKE, her head throbbed so badly she could scarcely open her eyes, and someone was demanding she wake up. Desperate to sink back into the comfort of oblivion, she batted away the annoying voice.

"Rose! Wake up. Are you all right?"

I would be if you'd let me sleep, she thought. Then memories of *why* her head ached so badly flooded in. Her eyelid creaked open and she beheld Will's concerned face hovering above her.

"They've taken Candace. A pair of...of men sent by Edward Merker. We fought them, but they dragged her away." She tried to rise and blackness swirled at the edges of her vision. Touching her forehead, her fingers came away with blood.

"Shh. You're hurt. You must rest. When I arrived the door was open and you were lying unconscious." Will, crouched beside her, laid her gently back on the floor.

It spun and nausea almost overtook her. "This is worse. Help me to sit. We have to—"

He interrupted, "I will get a cloth to staunch the wound and take you to my physician."

"I'll be all right, but Miss Sweet's situation is dire. Heaven knows what Merker will do once she's back in his clutches. Help me sit," Rose insisted.

Will carefully guided her upright, then fetched a glass of water and a cloth for her head.

Rose sipped gratefully, while telling in greater detail about the encounter with Merker's men. "We have to do something!"

"I'll handle it. Once I'm certain you're all right, I will deal with this Mr. Merker." With clenched jaw and steely eyes, mild-mannered William Carmody looked quite dangerous.

Rose felt too weak to argue. Truthfully, it was a relief to have Will take charge. He pressed the damp cloth to her head and went to telephone his physician.

Rose rested her eyes, and listened to the exchange from a sleepy distance.

Seconds later, Will returned to her side. "I was not able to reach him, but will drive you to the hospital for treatment."

Rose forced the fog away. "No. A doctor would only dispense an aspirin for the pain. We must go to Merker's home right now and demand her release."

"We have legal grounds," Will pointed out. "And are you certain that is where these thugs have taken her?"

"I don't know, but it is a good guess. We can't rely on a constable for help. We must rescue her," Rose wailed. "Please don't argue.

Will nodded curtly. "Right. I shall go then. But you must remain here."

"I will not. Two of us might stand a better chance, and I wish to be there for Candace." Her friend might even now be suffering intimate physical abuse at the hands of her caretaker.

Will did not argue further, but lifted her body in his arms and rose as if she weighed nothing. He carried her through the open doorway and did not set her on her feet until they were beside his motorcar, where he helped her inside.

As he drove toward the address Rose gave him, they maintained silence. Rose had managed to sound confident in convincing him of the urgency of helping Candace, but how would they gain entry into Merker's house if he didn't want them there?

When Will drew up in front of the residence, he addressed Rose with a severe expression. "I will go to the door. *You* will remain in the vehicle. If the man calls a constable, you aren't likely to be arrested since you will not have trespassed."

Arrested! The word brought her to earth with a jolt, as she realized what he sacrificed by offering his aid. "What do you intend to do?"

"Free Miss Sweet," he replied grimly, then got out of the vehicle and closed the door.

Rose watched his tall figure stride up the steps to the front door of a townhouse in a row of respectable homes. Lights shone from the windows, but no one answered the door after Will rang the bell. Perhaps the staff had been given instructions to ignore any visitors that evening.

What might the servants think of a young woman carried unconscious to her bedroom and locked in, if that is where she was? Just how dangerous were these thugs, and did they possess firearms? She could not sit idly by while Will walked into potential danger alone. Rose found a closed umbrella with a stout handle beneath the seat. She grabbed it up, ready to go to his aid.

Just then the front door finally opened and light spilled out to illuminate Will on the stoop. The fellow who had answered said something then began to close the door.

Will put his shoulder into it and shoved his way inside.

Heart pounding, Rose gripped the umbrella tightly and let herself out of the automobile to follow him—illegal entry be damned!

CHAPTER SEVENTEEN

WILL FELT LIKE a character in some detective novel, performing actions almost without conscious thought. The hallmarks of everyday Will were weighing options, wavering, and second guessing. Tonight, he was a fellow who pushed aside butlers and forged his way into another man's home. What would he do next?

"Miss Sweet. Are you here?" he called loudly.

"Please, sir. I must ask you to leave." The harried man stepped in front of Will to bar his passage.

"Stand aside," Will snarled. "If this young lady is being detained against her will and you are a part of it, you will be implicated in the crime."

He had no idea if this was true, but the butler collapsed like sails without wind and let him pass. Out of the corner of his eye, Will saw him slink toward the servants' door to downstairs.

"Mr. Merker! Edward Merker," Will shouted. "Show yourself, sir."

Instead of the house's owner, two very strong and capable looking chaps descended the stairs toward the grand hallway. One, as tall as Will and, broad across the shoulders, had his hand in his jacket pocket as if he might produce a pistol. His shorter partner's crooked nose and scarred eyebrow suggested he knew how to fight.

Will sometimes boxed with Guy, but he'd never laid a finger on anyone with the intent to cause damage. But his hands knew what to do, fingers beginning to curl into fists at the sight of the men who'd left Rose unconscious.

"Get out!" the tall fellow demanded.

Will took a moment to push his glasses firmly into place and take a breath. "I will speak to Mr. Merker," he said with uncompromising authority.

His partner scowled. "He says to throw you out of the house."

Will stalked forward. "I will not leave without Miss Sweet."

"Don't know who yer talkin' about," the fellow lied.

The pair had reached the foot of the stairs and split up, approaching him from either side like a pair of menacing dogs. He could not observe both, so Will concentrated on the man with the potential gun, while attempting to keep the other in his peripheral vision.

"Whatever Merker has paid you, I will double it if you leave now. No need to come to blows or for the police to become involved." Now *that* sounded like the peacekeeping Will he knew.

The stocky chap edged closer. "Get the 'ell out right now. This is family business and none o' yours."

Blood roared through Will's veins like a steam locomotive. This was happening.

He was about to—he charged the boxer, running his shoulder into his chest to knock him backward. Then he landed a surprise punch on that crooked nose. Blood spurted.

Will whirled around to ensure the other fellow hadn't drawn a weapon, only to see the astonishing sight of Rose running toward the man with an umbrella leveled like a lance. She howled like a Valkyrie and jabbed the sharp point into the tall man's side.

He cried out and grabbed the umbrella, jerking it from her hands. Will had but a second to see Rose seize a huge vase from a pedestal, and hurl it at the man. Then he returned his attention to the boxer, who'd recovered from the injury to his nose. The lower half of his face masked in blood, the man darted in to deliver a sharp blow to Will's stomach.

Breath left him. He wheezed and struggled to inhale. Meanwhile, his opponent rained a series of punches to his face and drove him down to the floor.

Will landed on all fours, using one arm to protect his head from the barrage. The speed and precision of the blows made it hard to fight back.

This man kicked Rose! End him! His ferocious alter ego ordered.

Will dug deep to find enough strength to match the other man's skill. Expecting little resistance, his opponent had drawn too near. When Will reared up, the back of his head connected with the underside of the fellow's jaw.

The boxer staggered backward as Will lunged to his feet. He leaped toward the man, his superior height and weight knocking the off-balance fighter to the ground. Will straddled his body and began to pummel his face like the bag at the gymnasium where he and Hardy practiced boxing. Thank god, Guy had dragged him there when Will did not wish to go.

Rage fueled him as he beat his opponent into submission. *I might kill him. I might very well kill him.* It took that realization to make Will halt his fist in mid-air and allow his fists to go slack.

With his antagonist no longer a threat, Will hurried to face the other enemy. He climbed off the unconscious boxer, and turned to find Rose standing over the man who lay amidst the shards of the broken urn.

She poked at the fellow's still form with the umbrella and looked up to meet Will's gaze. "I don't think he's dead."

He nodded. "That's good. But give him another hit to make sure he stays out cold."

Rose nodded, delivering a vigorous whack to her fallen adversary.

After that, they both looked toward the stairs. Up there, somewhere, Candace Sweet needed their rescue. Will nudged the boxer with his toe. The man didn't even groan. Will decided he wasn't likely to regain consciousness any time soon.

Together, he and Rose headed upstairs.

The house was not overly large and there were not many bedrooms. On either side of the hallway, Will and Rose tested door knobs, all unlocked, no room containing Candace or her guardian.

When a knob would not turn beneath her hand, Rose leaned close to the door. "Candace, are you in there? It's Rose."

If she were inside, the young woman was unable to reply, either unconscious or with a weapon held upon her. Not knowing what this Merker even looked like, Will imagined a mustachioed villain from a stage melodrama with a knife to her throat.

You've invaded the man's home. Too late to worry about legality now, Alter-Ego Will pointed out. The lock wouldn't budge without a key, so Will took his umbrella from Rose and wedged the tip below the bottom pin of one hinge. Many hard taps later, the bolt came free of the hinge.

Will repeated the process with the other hinges, while Rose continued to talk through the door. "Edward Merker, if you've harmed Miss Sweet, you *will* be held accountable. If not, I suggest you surrender her to us now."

WITH THE HINGES freed, Will just managed to pry the door from its frame and pull it open.

The moment there was space enough to fit, Rose charged into the room. "What have you done to 'er, bloody wanker?"

Will let go of his burden and entered to find Rose facing Edward Merker. The man bore no weapon and appeared a surprisingly average fellow with such nondescript features one would not recall him two seconds after leaving his presence. With thinning, light brown hair and pale blue eyes, he was of medium height and build, clothed in a brown tweed suit.

He might not hold a knife to Miss Sweet's throat, but the young woman lay on the bed behind him, unconscious and tied to the bedposts.

If Merker was terrified at the sight of them, he barely displayed it, instead adopting a tone of put-upon annoyance as if inconvenient visitors had arrived to spoil his tea time. "I must ask that you leave. You are not welcome here."

Rose pushed past him to lean over Candace. She felt for a pulse in her wrist, before starting to loosen the knots.

Merker's composure crumbled at the edges as Will advanced on him. His voice quavered. "The police will be on their way. My butler will have telephoned them."

"What would you tell them about Miss Sweet's condition; brought here against her will, sedated, and restrained?"

"A little laudanum to soothe her nerves was necessary. And restraint was the only option lest she hurt herself," he replied. "I've done nothing wrong. It is my duty to care for my ward, a sacred vow to a friend which I have fulfilled for years. She has never lacked for anything, nor will she. I intend to marry her, you see, and continue to protect her from the world—and even herself, if that is necessary, the poor child."

"Enough!" Will roared so loudly his throat ached. "You will allow her to leave with us, Mr. Merker. And you must swear not to trouble her again."

"Who precisely are you to make demands?" the fellow adopted false bravado like a rat backed into a corner.

"Lord Carmody. Do you recognize the name?" Adding a title gave his words more authority to cow this fellow into submission. "In addition to acknowledging Miss Sweet's autonomy, you will relinquish control of her inheritance immediately. No court battles. No diverting the money to hidden accounts. Every penny owed will be released to her this very day. Is that understood?"

Will held his breath, praying his gambit and stellar acting would do the trick. If he'd assessed the fellow correctly, he would acquiesce to a perceived superior.

Merker had retreated so his back was to the bureau. "She is my ward. I have every right to guide her as I see fit. Any court would agree."

"Not once they learn you drugged her and tied her up to force her into marriage." Rose had loosened the ropes and now chafed feeling into Candace's wrists. "How much did you give her? She's limp as a corpse."

Will moved nearer to loom over Merker. "I know that the young lady's father was your superior and you forged the signature on his so-called will." He spoke as if it were fact rather than Rumsfield's estimation. "There was no one to question the legality of the document then, but *I* am here now to contest the will. Would you truly wish to go against all of my resources in court?"

The man's gaze darted around, searching for an avenue of escape. The mere strength of Will's resolve deflated him. "All I ever wanted was to protect the girl, such a darling little thing as a child and now a lovely young lady. But she has become too opinionated in her years away from home. She no longer recognizes that I know what is best for her."

"Sedating and restraining her sounded like the best cure for that," Will said dryly.

"Until she came to her senses, yes," Merker replied quite seriously.

Rose had succeeded in rousing Candace to drowsy consciousness and now called for Will's help. "Between us we can help her walk. Let us get her out of this horrible place."

But he was not ready to retreat while Merker feared his threats. Later the fellow might realize his promises of legal action were hollow. "Before we leave, I will have a signed affidavit from you agreeing to immediately relinquish both Miss Sweet and her inheritance. My solicitor will review all documents and finish the matter tomorrow. If you defy me, I swear to have you prosecuted for forgery at the very least—fraud and kidnapping at the worst. Do you understand me?"

Amazing what bluster and authority could do.

Merker was reduced to obsequious fawning. "No need to become involved in a legal battle. As my ward is nearly of age, I will release her inheritance. I have not misused the money, but have, in fact, invested and expanded her holdings."

"Now all of it is hers, ya right bloody bastard. You'll not control her any longer," Rose helped Candace sit upright and slid an arm around her back.

Will exhaled a long breath. It was time to get out of the house before those thugs regained consciousness. But he would not leave without Merker's concession in hand. Finding some writing paper on the bureau, Will continued to intimidate Merker until the man had written and signed the requested affidavit.

"Let that be an end to it. If you bother Miss Sweet again, there will be the very devil to pay, I promise you." Will snatched the document from the Merker and stashed it in his pocket, then hurried to aide Rose with woozy Miss Sweet. Together, they propelled her from the room, the walk already seeming to clear the effects of chloroform chased by laudanum from her system.

Will glanced back at Mr. Merker to see the diminished man standing in the doorway like a child whose favorite toy had been snatched away.

They guided her down the stairs, bypassing the sprawled bodies of the two agents who would not halt their progress. Nearly to the foyer, Will observed eyes watching from the entry to the servants' domain.

At his notice, the door quickly closed. No one came out to impede them.

"Home free," he muttered after they had exited the house.

Rose drew Candace's slumped body straighter by tugging at the arm around her shoulders. "I can't believe you pulled it off. You were magnificent! Anyone would have yielded."

"I wish I'd tried something sooner and saved the pair of you from a harrowing ordeal," Will panted as he bundled Miss Sweet into the auto's back seat. "It never occurred to me to cut straight through legal action for faster results."

"And you believe what you made him sign will be sufficient for him to leave her be?" Rose covered Miss Sweet with her own coat and smoothed her hair as the woman drifted back to sleep.

"Legally, I believe so. Jennings will sew it up tight. One can only hope he will not hound her after this." Will sat behind the wheel and started the engine. "I will stop at my physician's home. Both of you should be seen to."

"I'm already feeling better, except for a headache, and it may be best to simply allow Candace to sleep off the drug. If either of us wakes in the morning worse for wear, that will be soon enough to go to a doctor."

"I won't leave you two alone," Will said firmly. No matter how strong Rose's opinions, he would be Gibraltar on this point. He held up his hand to stop her arguing. "Merker might send his goons again. I will stand guard till morning and remain on the premises until I feel certain you are both completely safe."

With a nod of concession, Rose closed her mouth and relaxed into the seat.

Now that the drama was over, Will had time to recall his overwhelming sense of horror upon seeing Rose lying on the floor, a puddle of blood beneath her head. For one galvanizing instant he was certain she was dead, and promised God he would do anything, give anything, if she were only alive.

Now he thought, *I love her. I am absolutely, irrefutably in love with this woman. And I must do whatever it takes to convince her we can live happily ever after—if only she will allow me the chance.*

CHAPTER EIGHTEEN

BY THE TIME they reached the shop, Candace was alert enough to speak. She regarded them both after Rose helped her into bed. "Thank you from the bottom of my heart. Thank you both for your friendship. You have saved me in so many ways."

"You'll be safe now. He should not bother you again. Rest. You have nothing to fear." Rose tucked in the covers and she and Will left the room.

He appeared huge and unexpected standing in the middle of her meager flat. Rose found herself wanting to apologize for its paucity—as if that mattered, as if Will were the type of man who would mind. Instead she said, "Thank you for coming to our aid. You were nothing less than heroic tonight."

"As were you," he replied. "When you charged in brandishing that umbrella, I would have hated to be on the pointy end of your fury."

"I can have a bit of a temper when my friends have been attacked and locked up. What a disgusting toad!"

"Indeed. I still fear for you both, which is why I insist on remaining here to make certain you both are safe." He glanced around the room. "I will, of course, sit in a chair downstairs."

"You will not. If you insist on guarding us, and I can tell there is no use arguing, then you must be made at least a little comfortable." Rose gathered cushions and blankets to form a pallet on the floor. "Tea?"

she asked, although her head was pounding and she wanted nothing more than to relax at last.

Will shook his head. "You are exhausted after your ordeal. Sleep now, and we will discuss everything in the morning."

Within half an hour of arriving home, Rose lay in bed, listening to Will's shifting and breathing on the other side of the wall. He might rest more comfortably in her bed, their bodies warmly pressed together. He would hold her and, after a bit, begin to touch her—just there. Her hand found the spot. And then…

How was it possible to have sensual inclinations after the terrible events of the evening? Yet the danger and violence seemed to have ignited passion. She should be considering Candace's wellbeing, but thoughts of tiptoeing from her room join Will beneath the knitted afghan danced in her head. Honestly, such wanton notions! Rose removed her hand from between her legs and rolled onto her side, determined to sleep.

WHEN SHE OPENED her eyes, it was to daylight seeping under the window sash.

Drowsy thoughts warmed her for a moment before she bolted upright. Her supplier would have come to deliver the flowers by now and she had not been there to answer the door. She would be forced to make do with yesterday's slightly drooping flowers. Her reputation would suffer and she'd be out of business before she could say Jack Sprat.

Rose leaped from the bed and into a dress. She combed out her hair and rolled it into a simple twist. Low voices drifted from the flat, Will and Candace speaking together.

When Rose joined them, Candace appeared refreshed in a daffodil yellow frock, and with a smile on her wan face. Will caught sight of Rose and he poured her a cup. "Good morning. How is your head today?"

"Nothing an aspirin powder won't cure," she replied. "What about you, Candace? Feeling any better?"

Candace's brown eyes sparkled. "Much better, and I have both of you to thank for it. When I think of how things might have gone, my gratitude will never cease. It seems as if I will soon be completely free of Edward Merker at last."

"I am so glad. Now, you must rest today and recover I should go down and sort out what to do about the flowers. Perhaps it is not too late to get something fresh from the market."

"Your daily order is already here. I helped the farmer carry the flowers inside," Will said calmly. "Sit and have the eggs I made for you. While I go and put the flowers in their display buckets, you and Miss Sweet catch up."

"But you haven't had a proper rest. You slept on a floor last night. I really can't sit while you do my work."

"You may for a few minutes. Please don't argue." Will stood and guided Rose into the chair he'd occupied. It was still warm.

After he left, Rose inhaled the calming fragrance of tea rising from her steaming cup. "Do you still feel dizzy or have any residual effects?"

"None at all. Truly, I am well and happier than I have ever been. In France, I was as constrained by Madame Brodeur's strict rules as I had been at home. For the first time in my life, I may do whatever I please with no one controlling me."

"Whatever you decide to do with your life, I'm certain it will be great, although I do hope you'll remain my assistant for a time."

"Of course! Mr. Carmody promises he will make certain the legalities of attaining my rights are sorted out, so I will certainly help in the shop today. That Mr. Carmody of yours is a very remarkable gentleman."

"He's not *my* Mr. Carmody, but yes, he is a good friend."

"More than a friend I think. He is clearly in love with you." Candace smiled.

"No. He may have some romantic ideal of who I am, but he doesn't really know me."

"I think he does, and I believe you are in love with him too. Why would you fight against it?"

"You are not naïve, Candace. You know a gentleman of his station could never marry a commoner like me."

"If ever there was a man who didn't give a fig about bloodline or society's censure, it is he. Come now, Rose, you are a suffragette who believes in equality. Why would you rate yourself as somehow lower than Mr. Carmody?"

Rose shrugged. "His family would never accept me, and if he ever met mine, he'd run away screaming. The two of us together would be like a dandelion and orchid in the same bouquet—just wrong."

"Both are plants which require water, adequate light, and proper soil to grow. They are the same beneath their differences and each beautiful in a different way. Don't allow a chance at happiness to slip away due to a lack of faith in your worth." Candace touched Rose's hand. "I could not bear to see you unhappy, and I fear you will be if you don't open your heart to the love Mr. Carmody has to give. You deserve him, and he deserves you."

Rose squeezed the hand stretched out in kindness, but offered no reply. "I must open the store. You may join me when you are ready."

IN THE SHOP, Will crouched to fill the last of the flower bins. He'd arranged by hue so the blooms ranged from pale yellow to a deep blue across the risers.

"You've an eye for color. Thank you so much for rising early for the vendor."

"I almost shook you awake as I was worried you had become comatose. Are you quite certain I cannot take you to my physician?"

Rose tapped her aching forehead. "Right as rain and any bruising is hidden by my hair, so the customers won't be aghast."

He rose and wiped his wet hands on his trousers. Yesterday's trousers. The poor man hadn't had an opportunity to change to fresh clothing.

"You must go home," she commanded, then realized he might misunderstand. "I mean, you haven't had any solid sleep or a chance to wash up."

"Are you certain you don't need my help here?"

"Candace will be down shortly. I don't believe we need to fear Mr. Merker or his agents during the daylight hours. I do thank you again for becoming so involved. You didn't have to."

"Of course, I did. I behaved as I would for any friend in trouble." He picked several leaves off his sleeve before speaking again. "But I must tell you, Rose, I do not really wish to remain friends with you."

"Oh." It felt as if her stomach had been kicked rather than her head. Being summoned from his home in the night to punch and threaten people had been too much for him, of course. Why would he want a friend who would drag him into such violent drama?

"I see," she replied. "I understand."

"No. I don't believe you do." He grasped her arms and faced her squarely. "I meant to say I don't wish to remain *merely* your friend. I told you it would be sufficient, but it isn't. I want so much more than that and I am no longer afraid to ask. Please you grant me the favor of being your beau, Miss Gardener. Allow me to court you properly and if, at the end of a month, you still cannot envision us together, I will walk away with no hard feelings."

"Oh, Will, you make it so hard to say no."

His mouth tightened. "All right. At least I've tried."

"Now you misunderstand me," she said. "You make it so hard to say no, that I will say 'yes' instead."

A thought occurred, an opportunity for him to truly understand how vastly different their worlds were. "Will you accompany me to my sister's wedding?"

His eyes opened wide, bright and eager. "Yes. Absolutely! When and where?"

CHAPTER NINETEEN

THE OLD CHURCH, wedged incongruously between a cemetery and a more recently built butcher's shop, could scarcely accommodate both the Barnes and Gardener extended families. In addition to the immediate families, there were aunts, uncles, cousins, half-relations, and friends from the neighborhood on both sides. Ongoing feuds of one sort or another separated them into various clusters who shot bitter looks at one another. Insults and arguments flew back and forth across the aisle before the minister arrived to temporarily quell the seething resentments.

Rose kept glancing at her escort to gauge his reaction to the noisy crowd assembled for a sacred occasion.

Will's lips twitched as her brother Danny, sitting beside him in the pew, muttered about an enemy, "Bloody arsehole! I'll see him dead if he crosses me again." And Will could hardly contain his amusement when Dale's wife Madge cuffed her son on the side of the head to keep him from making paper airplanes from the hymnal pages.

Please start. Please be over soon. Rose prayed with folded hands. Her wish was granted as Alice Chauncey played Arietta and Dad up the aisle on a wheezing organ.

Her sister looked truly lovely in her pink ensemble, but far too fresh and glowing to be marrying the grizzled Gus Barnes. He was nearly dashing in his uniform with freshly trimmed hair and beard, but so very much older than Arietta it made Rose grimace. The vows were dispensed with in short order and the guests raised a cheer at the kiss that sealed the union.

"Your sister is a beautiful bride," Will whispered. "She seems very happy."

"I pray she will be in the future as well," Rose said. "Wish I could tell you this is the end of it and we could leave now, but there's the reception yet to come."

"I'll be pleased to meet your family."

You won't be, she thought. But perhaps it wouldn't be as bad as she imagined. The heavy drinking wouldn't start till later in the day, so Dad might not be quite as belligerent or Mum as quick with the sly jabs at anyone who crossed her path. She would be sure to leave before they reached that point.

Hoorahs and good wishes lasted about as long as it took for Arietta and her groom to go down the aisle, greeting people on the right and left on their way. One could almost believe the good nature would last, but truce flags went down as soon as everyone left the church.

Outside the building, Danny resumed squabbling with his one-time rival Job Barnes, Gus's younger brother. Their fight quickly escalated to blows, forcing other guests to pull them apart, which naturally led to more fisticuffs on the side.

"What's the argument about?" Will asked, watching the brawling with interest.

"Years ago my brother and Job were stepping out with the same girl," Rose explained. "She's long since wed someone else, yet the two continue to fight bitterly over the betrayal."

"Who's yer fancy man, Rosie?" Madge butted into their conversation, extending her hand toward Will. "How d'ya do? I'm Dale's wife."

"So pleased to meet you, Mrs. Gardener." He bowed over her hand.

Madge gave Rose a wide-eyed expression of shock above his head.

"Cor, what manners! And what a fine suit. Looks like ya landed yerself a gent here. Good for you, Rose."

"Sally's dunking her doll in the baptismal font. Might want to look into that." Rose directed her sister-in-law away. After Madge went inside the church, Rose said, "I apologize for her rude manners."

"Nonsense. She was very complimentary," Will said smoothly. "Now, may I meet your parents?"

There was no avoiding it. Arietta and her new husband had already left for the hall rented for the occasion. As Mum and Dad approached, Rose pasted on a smile.

"It was a beautiful wedding. You outdid yourself decorating the church, Mum."

"No thanks to you who couldn't be bothered to come early."

Rose had spent much of the morning helping Arietta dress and arranging her coiffure prior to Will meeting her at the church. She ignored the barb. "Mother, Father, I should like to introduce you to Mr. William Carmody. Mr. Carmody, Mr. and Mrs. Peter Gardener."

Will smiled and bowed slightly "How do you do? I'm very pleased to meet the parents of such a lovely and accomplished woman as Miss Rose."

Mother sized him up as if he were a zoo animal, noted his genteel manner and fine suit—far better than the one the groom had worn, and adopted her best imitation of an upper crust accent. "Pleased to meet you as well. Rose has not mentioned you before. Do tell us something about yourself. Who are your people?"

If taken aback by her questioning, Will did not betray it. "Lord Horace and Lady Gwyneth Carmody. I was introduced to your daughter by a mutual friend, Mr. Guy Hardy. Her direct manner and strength of character immediately impressed me."

"Always was a stubborn one, our Rosie, an' too proud for 'er own good." Dad, in the jovial phase of the day's drinking, clapped Will on the back as if he were an old friend. "Drink to my daughter's weddin' day, Carmody." He offered the bottle in his fist.

Will politely refused. "No thank you. I have a bit of a sore throat and wouldn't want to share any illness."

"Then you'll drink with me when we get to the party. A full barrel awaits and a spread the likes of which ya ain't never seen. No one can say I didn't see me daughter off right," he announced grandly.

"I'll be sure to enjoy a beer then."

Rose touched Dad's arm to stop him from taking another pull on the gin bottle. "Time for that later. Best move everyone along, don't you think?"

He jerked his arm away. "Don't tell me what to do, gal. Like I said, ya never did mind yer betters or know yer place."

"She's right, Pete," Mum interrupted, anxious to quell him before he frightened off her daughter's wealthy beau, a potential resource to be mined in the future. She dropped an unnatural and unnecessary curtsey to Will. "Pleased to meet you, sir. I pray we will see much more of you in the days to come."

Not if I can bloody help it. After they'd walked away, Rose exhaled the breath she'd been holding. "My parents. Do you understand why I was not anxious for you to meet them, or any of these people?" she indicated the dispersing crowd.

"If I didn't know better, I'd say you were a snob, Miss Gardener," Will countered. "They are a boisterous lot, certainly, but not bad at heart I'm sure."

"If by boisterous you mean coarse and loud." She shook her head as Madge passed by dragging her dripping daughter away from the baptismal font. Her scolding was peppered with expletives that made Rose wince.

"I don't mean to judge them," she continued. "But really, do you *see* now? No one ever talks quietly here when a shout will do, or applies reason or calmness to solve an issue. It seems tempers are always on the verge of breaking and there is no peace to be had. Is it any wonder, I wanted to escape or that I was immediately drawn to a soft-spoken man like you?"

Will took her hand. "I do understand, but wish to point out that squabbles, feuds and criticisms occur in the very best families. Only the insults are delivered in backhanded compliments and disdain is masked by good manners. I have attended events at which royal family members were present and witnessed seething yet repressed anger. So-called 'polite' society's way is to deliver sharp thorns in a bouquet of well-wishes."

His cool hazel gaze soothed her irritation like balm and prompted a different sort of internal fretting. If only they could be alone to explore that anxious feeling.

"Now shall we go to the party?" Will asked.

Rose nodded.

SEVERAL HOURS INTO the festivities, with the food gone and the keg getting low, the dancing began. Jigs, reels and foxtrots filled the union hall which reeked of smoke from years of workers gathering to dispute their wages, wait out strikes, or socialize during the good times.

Arietta's hair had tumbled and strands stuck to her sweating forehead. A growing rip separated one side of her bodice seam, but her face glowed as Sergeant Gus Barnes swung her around. She appeared happier than Rose had ever seen her. Perhaps this match *was* the perfect one for her sister.

"Would you care to dance?" Will held out his hand. "I'm not much good at it, but I'm game to try."

The reel had ended and the fiddle struck up a waltz. "Anyone can waltz," Rose pointed out. "Step, step, slide." She reached high to rest her palm on his shoulder, and a thrill quivered through her as he slid his hand around her waist.

Then she was airborne. Not literally as he did not quite sweep her off her feet, but with every glide and turn, her spirit lifted higher. This was the sort of romantic feeling she had yearned for but not found in any chap she'd stepped out with. This was *more* than romance for the feelings tied into the giddy sensation were powerful enough to take her outside of herself.

Love. I am in love with William Carmody and he appears to be in love with me. The beautiful crystalline thought filled her mind. Any worries for the future no longer mattered, for this moment of pure happiness was sufficient to last a lifetime.

When at length the song ended, Rose and Will remained locked together, breathing in unison, gazing into each other's eyes. He did not let her go, nor did she want him to.

"A toast!" someone yelled and delivered a speech punctuated by belches.

Rose exhaled shakily. "Well… I believe you lied about your accomplishments, because you are a very fine dancer."

He slowly slid his hand from her waist. "I was hardly aware of what I was doing. Holding you felt so natural. Rose, I know we have only just met, but might I ask if you would consider—"

"There you are!" Her father boomed, interrupting. "Said you'd throw back a drink with me. 'Ere you go." He thrust a full glass of beer at Will which sloshed over the rim and wet his sleeve. "Drink up. Drink up. It's a party."

"Thank you, Mr. Gardener," Will replied with good grace, taking the glass from the drunk's unsteady hand.

"So, just how rich are you? Enough to keep my girl in the manner she deserves?"

"Dad, stop!" Humiliation burned through Rose like a fever. She could not bear to look at Will.

"Shut up, you!" her father snarled, his expression set in the belligerent scowl she knew too well. "This is business. If you and Lord Muckety-Muck are going to shack up, 'im an' me need to make an agreement."

"You're drunk. Be quiet." *Before you say something even worse.* Although what could possibly be worse than the implication she was a prostitute.

"Tis a father's duty to make sure 'is girls is cared for." He waved an arm to indicate Arietta, beer spattering across the floor. "Yer sister's soldier ain't bad, but seems you done her one better. But ya can't count on the man's goodwill. You gotta lock in a figure."

"Mr. Gardener, I'm afraid you misunderstand my intentions toward your daughter," Will stopped Dad's yammering with icy control. "We will not co-habit unless married, and that is my full intention, given time to court her."

Dad's bloodshot eyes went wide. "You ain't bloody serious. I don't believe it. You'll use her an' leave 'er in a family way no matter what fancy promises ya make now. Fellers like you don't marry gals from Spitalfields. I'm 'ere to see my daughter gets what's comin' to 'er. Tis only right."

"Dad!" Rose nearly howled. "Stop talking!"

He barely glanced at her as he yelled. "I said shut up. This is men's business."

Will's tone went even more glacial as he spoke slowly. "I must insist you not speak to Rose in that manner. Nor will I tolerate your suggestion that she act as my paid companion. You need not speak on her behalf. This young woman has built a business without any aid from you. She is capable of managing her life and making all decisions concerning her future without your interference."

The red-faced drunk raised a shaky finger and jabbed it toward the distinguished gentleman who towered over him. "You—"

"No more disrespect, please, Mr. Gardener. Am I understood?" Will thundered, but in a low rumble like a distant storm. There would be lightning, hail, and torrential downpour if it arrived. "I would not wish for Rose to be permanently alienated from family, so I will attempt to remain forbearing. But I warn you, my patience is near its end."

Rose caught her breath. In an alcohol haze, her father was beyond reason enough to fight men much larger than he. Any second he might take a swing at Will.

Instead his fury abruptly abated like a beaten pit bull slinking from the ring. He even bowed his head. "Point taken, mate. My misunderstanding. Wouldn't want to offend a future son-in-law, eh?"

Her father held out his hand, and for the first time Rose noticed how gnarled his fingers were. Dad had become an old man, weak and whining rather than the dominating figure of her youth. He was pathetic.

Will did not hesitate to shake. "I'm happy we understand one another and pray there will be no further discord in the future, Mr. Gardener. I'm certain we both wish Rose nothing but happiness."

"Yes. Yes, sir. That's all I ever wanted for my kids."

"Then we shall drink together and speak no more of the matter." Will took a small sip from the glass, although his tight-lipped expression suggested he would rather pour its contents over her father's head.

"Hear, hear," Dad agreed before finishing the rest of his beer. With a mumbled excuse, he sidled away.

Rose had no words. Her mind was a stew of embarrassment, anger, surprise, and satisfaction at how neatly Will had handled her troublesome parent. She'd never seen anyone vanquish her dad with words alone.

Will found a table on which to set the glass, and visibly shook off his tension before facing Rose again. "There might be some interesting holiday dinners ahead for us, that is, if you'll agree to marry me."

"How is it possible his rudeness did not put you off? And how can you want to marry me? Can you imagine my interview with your family would go much better?"

Will put his hands on her shoulders and peered into her face.

"How can you imagine that anything can stop us from having what we want? The most important question is do *you* share my feelings even a little?"

He paused, frowning. "I am aware I've moved too quickly from first meeting to declaration. The trouble is I have waited years to meet a woman I would want to spend my life with. I had accustomed myself to the idea of being forever alone. So when I met you and a light switched on inside me, I could not bear to turn it off again. I know what I want without hesitation or reservation. It is you, Miss Rose Gardener, if you'll have me. Given more time, do you think you might come to love me and accept my proposal?"

She'd dithered back and forth concerning her feelings for Will for days now, but when she cut through the brambles of indecision, what was left? A single perfectly formed rose.

"Yes," she blurted as realization dawned. "Yes, Will. I feel the same strong feeling for you! I can't think why I fought so hard against it. Whatever challenges face us, be it our families or society, we will overcome. I will continue to see you, and one day soon, I expect to accept your proposal."

If the expression "beaming with joy" had an illustration, it would be Will's expression at her words. He slid his hands down her arms to grasp her hands and press them to his lips. "My darling, you have made me the happiest of men."

Rose laughed for if she tried to speak the knot in her throat would come undone and she would start sobbing. Damn the wedding guests or what anyone thought, she threw her arms around his neck and pulled his face to her level so she could kiss him.

Will's arms tightened hard around her, holding her fast against him.

As the wedding couple left the party to well-wishes and off-color remarks about the wedding night, Rose knew more than one set of vows had been exchanged that day. She did not trust Arietta's and Gus's would be kept, but she had no doubt hers and Will's would.

CHAPTER TWENTY

STANDING IN THE center of the conservatory, Will pressed his hands into the small of his back and stretched. He'd been stooped over for too long planting, but the results were worth a little pain. Seedlings covered every bit of the beds, leaving just enough room around them to grow. One perfect little orange tree fresh from the nursery served as the focal point for the room. The transplant had not affected the sapling, for the leaves were still green and healthy. If cultivated carefully, by next year it might bloom and bear fruit. Rather like his relationship with Rose—the most important feature in the garden.

He gazed fondly at his beloved, dirt smudged across her forehead where she'd wiped away sweat, dress filthy as a chimney sweep's garb. She could not have been more beautiful with her bright red hair catching a ray of sunlight on this overcast blustery day. His garden had only come alive through the grace of Rose. She was the instrument of his growth, as well as that of the greenhouse plants. He would love her forever for bringing life into his life.

As if feeling his gaze upon her, Rose looked up from where she knelt in a puddle of green skirts. Her smile made his heart swell until it might burst. "What do you think? Is it everything you imagined?"

"And more." Will let his lingering gaze signal that he meant her presence. He offered a hand to pull Rose to her feet.

"I thought perhaps a bench would go just there." She pointed. "Or perhaps two garden chairs with a small table. What do you think?"

"One large bed might be more comfortable if we are to spend any length of time here," he teased daringly.

"Mr. Carmody, you shock me. Reardon would be horrified if we became more familiar than what he has already witnessed."

"That was an unfortunate incident." Will recalled the day the butler had walked in on them kissing in the library. More than kissing, actually, as there were body parts exposed and hands in unseemly places. Admirably, Reardon had displayed no discomposure, merely announced tea and left the room.

"Honestly," Will continued. "I believe the old fellow adores you and will be quite happy when you are mistress here. Like my mother, he is simply content to see me settled at last."

"Your mother." Rose frowned. "You continue to say that, but I'm not at all certain it is true. She was painstakingly polite to me at dinner the other night, yet cold as a North wind."

"She will settle into the idea. Father thinks you are remarkable. I can tell, for I know how to read his silence. Rupert and Virginia seem taken with you as well, although they generally do not demonstrate interest in anything beyond their horses. And my nephews deemed you 'topping' and 'first rate.' You passed with high marks."

He drew her into his arms and kissed her lightly. "You are well-liked by my family, and loved by me." Another kiss, deeper and more lasting, underlined his statement.

Rose seemed to abandon her worries in the comfort of his arms. Will would never have imagined himself possessing the power to provide contentment and happiness to someone. It was the finest feeling in the world.

"I do love you," he whispered when his mouth was free.

"And I love you." She looked at him from so close, a full palette of blues was visible in her eyes. They were like diamonds reflecting only the blue light of the spectrum. How was it possible such an exquisite being could have fallen for him? But Will would not question it, merely accept with gratitude that, like her flowers, Rose had brought him to bloom.

Another kiss was interrupted by the clearing of a throat. Will released his almost fiancée.

"Lord and Lady Carmody have arrived and await you in the drawing room," Reardon announced.

"Here? Now? I'm a fright, and I've nothing to change into!" Rose exclaimed.

"Never mind your gown. Mother understands the rigors of gardening if anyone does, and their visit is unexpected," Will reassured her. "Wash up and I will meet you in the hallway to escort you into the drawing room. Please try to relax, Rose. You look perfect."

"This is no time for compliments. Can't you make excuses for me? I will see them another day when I am better prepared."

"I'd prefer you stay with me. Will you do that for me? We can show them the conservatory together."

She hesitated then regarded him seriously. "If it is important to you, then very well. I made it through dinner at their house. No doubt I'll survive this interview. For it *is* an interview, and not a casual visit. I expect them to have views concerning my background, and you should expect it too."

He nodded. "You are right, of course. Mother likely will have something to say. But I will be there to support you, and if you grow too distressed, you must give me a sign and I will end the conversation."

"How about this for the sign?" Rose pressed her nose up with one finger turning her saucy nose into a pig snout.

"Yes. I believe that will do." Will laughed at his sweetheart, who could deflect her fear with humor. He gave her a last embrace before letting go. "You are sunshine, Rose Gardener. Is it any wonder I love you?"

ROSE CHECKED HER reflection once more in the hallway mirror. There was little she could do about the stains on her skirt, but at least her hair was arranged in a neat bun and her face and hands were clean. She practiced smiling. *Good afternoon, your lordship and ladyship. So good to see you again.*

Will held her hand and led her to her doom.

Rose caught a breath before entering the drawing room where her prospective in-laws sat in chairs they must have occupied for many years. Probably Lord Carmody's grandparents' and great-grandparents' bums had occupied those same seats. And now an upstart threatened to claim one of them for her own.

Will gave her hand a squeeze as he went to kiss his mother's cheek. "What an unexpected surprise," he murmured. "What has brought you to town?"

"Business," his lordship said succinctly.

"And pleasure," Lady Carmody took over for him. "I wanted to see you, my dear, and I could not wait for your promised reveal of the finished conservatory. Might we view it today?"

Rose waited with her formal greeting trembling on her lips, but it seemed they were bypassing that. She might relax for a moment.

But only a moment, for now her ladyship turned to her. "Miss Gardener. It appears we have interrupted your work. Would *you* care to show me the room, while the men remain here to visit with one another?"

Will stood up. "Father and I will come with you. I had planned to show you both the renovation."

"Sit, son. We'll have a chat of our own and let the ladies go on about their business, eh? I'll take a look at the room another time."

Divided! Rose hadn't counted on that. The grand dame was going to get her alone and attempt to uproot the common weed from her son's garden. Her stomach churned at the thought, but then she began to grow angry. She'd spent too long fretting over the difference in their status and was finished worrying about that. Damned if she would yield to pressure, or give up the man she loved.

"It's all right, Will. I will show your mother what we've created together." Rose took the lead, a reminder to her ladyship that this was no longer her house. She felt the woman's gaze skewering her all the way to the greenhouse, but when she glanced at Lady Carmody, the woman wasn't looking at her at all.

Moving into the room and turning in a slow circle, Will's mother appeared overcome by emotion. "Oh my. This room was never so lovely or in such good condition. When I came here as a bride, the conservatory was already several generations old and had been terribly neglected. I put it to rights as best I could, but the repairs and changes Will has instituted are beyond anything I imagined. Well done. Now your work here is finished, what will you do?"

Her ladyship faced Rose, who prepared to do battle.

"Continue to cultivate the plants. And we thought we might place a bench underneath the orange tree." She specifically chose the word "we" to leave Lady Carmody in no doubt that Rose would continue to be part of the picture. "As it grows, the branches would shelter and the fruit provide a delightful scent."

"Yes. I can imagine they would." She paused. "And I can picture the pair of you enjoying the spot."

"You can?" Rose blurted before thinking.

"Yes, my dear. Actually, I envision it quite clearly." Lady Carmody paused before speaking again. "May I speak plainly?"

"I would like that."

"I must admit to trepidation upon our first meeting. Your sudden presence in my son's life was...unexpected to say the least. You sprang from seemingly nowhere and I could tell he was greatly enamored of you. My William was always a thoughtful, sensitive lad, who grew into a shy and self-contained man. I knew if he ever gave his heart and his trust it would be fully and without compromise. Such a man would be easy for a self-serving person to latch onto."

"I am not… I never…" Rose began to bluster.

Her ladyship held up a hand. "Please, allow me to finish. At dinner the other night I observed you closely and made note of your manner with William. I came to the conclusion that no one could feign the expression of glowing admiration I witnessed upon your face that evening. I believe now you mean my son no harm and truly love him."

"I do! It must seem mad to you. We've come to know each other so recently and our friendship developed so rapidly."

"Yes, it did," the older woman said dryly. "Very rapidly. But that is neither here nor there. The point is you have become a part of William's life. He clearly intends to wed you."

Now that it appeared she had Lady Carmody's blessing after all, Rose found herself spewing all of her own shortcomings. "I know my background is not what you would hope for. I fear I will never fit into your world. I don't know the proper protocol or who anyone in society is, or what is expected in any given situation. But I will do my best to emulate your behavior and make myself presentable on social occasions."

"Which is all one could hope for. My goodness, you are a loquacious girl, aren't you? Might I finish my thoughts?"

"Yes, of course. My apologies." Rose bit her bottom lip to keep from babbling any further.

"I merely wanted to point out that William is not the first man who has married outside his class—far outside his class—and whose wife successfully forged her way into society. Lady Baden Churchfield, for example, was once an actress. William has no interest in attending social events, so it should not be too difficult for you to maintain a low profile, as it were. Do you intend to keep your florist's?"

"I do. I love my business and will not give it up. I hope you do not see that as a problem."

"Not at all. The pair of you are already so unconventional, what difference could it make? There will be gossip regardless." Lady Carmody paused to stroke the freshly cut boards of the newly constructed worktable. "I should have been a gardener," she said more to herself than Rose. "After I gave up living in London for the Season and spent all my time in the estate gardens, I found my truest happiness. I was born to nurture growing things."

Rose held her breath, feeling as if she witnessed a private moment.

"It may seem of little consequence to an outsider, but my gardening club is everything to me. Being awarded a prize from the Royal Horticultural society for my hybrid was a dream come true."

Her ladyship appeared to shake off a dream and resumed her brisk manner of speaking. "Have you not noticed the rather large parcel standing in the corner?"

In fact, Rose had not, being far more concerned with this important meeting with her prospective mother-in-law. Now she looked toward the spot Lady Carmody indicated. Indeed, there was a parcel wrapped in brown paper resting on the flagstones.

"Open it."

Rose did as she was bid. Treating the gift with as much care as if it were a bomb, she carefully untapped the paper and pulled it open to reveal a small rosebush. She opened the paper further.

"Samuel watered the root ball before wrapping it in burlap, but the sooner you get them in the ground, the better," Lady Carmody advised.

Rose knelt to more closely study the leaves and spied one tiny bud still green and barely erupted. "Is this it? The *Lucinda May*?"

"No. It is a venerable variety the locals grow, one that will remain contained and not take too much space. As I mentioned, I am keen to save heritage roses from extinction. I pray this bush will serve to remind you of the importance of maintaining some aspects of our past."

Rose looked up at the woman, whose voice trembled and eyes glistened. "Yes, your ladyship. I will remain mindful of the Carmody heritage and preserve it to the best of my ability," she pledged.

"Good. Now, let us plant that poor uprooted bush. If you choose a spot, I will help you."

A WHILE LATER, with his parents gone and the quiet of the conservatory broken only by the wind pelting raindrops against the panes, Rose and Will settled together on a chair he'd dragged in from the library. It was sufficient to accommodate two, so long as they sat very close together.

Rose rested her head against Will's chest, listening to the rain and to her beloved's even breathing. "What did your father have to say?" she asked presently.

"Very little. It was obvious Mother told him to have a talk with me, so he did it begrudgingly. He told me marrying a strong-willed woman was both a great blessing and a splinter embedded in one's heart for life. He suggested I save putting my foot down for only the most important occasions. That was the sum total of his advice."

She laughed. "Would you put your foot down some day? What if I don't care to obey your commands?"

"Then I imagine we will find a solution midway between our opposing points of view. Civilization demands it. What about Mother? Did she give you too much trouble?"

"Actually, no. I think you were right and she doesn't despise me. I would even venture to say she believes I am a good match for you. The last thing she said before we rejoined you and your father was 'Continue to make my son happy and I will embrace you as a daughter.' Isn't that sweet?"

Now Will chuckled. "When you meet Penny, you should ask how that works for her. My sister and mother have had rows that sent the dogs slinking from the house in fear."

Silence fell once more. Rose idly measured the length of her hands against Will's, then entwined their fingers together. It had been nearly three weeks since they had secured Candace's freedom and become unofficially engaged. Will had promised a ring of Rose's choice when she was ready to shop for one.

"Would you read a chapter of Pan to me?" Rose requested after a bit. "I adore the sound of your voice."

"Given that sort of compliment, how can I refuse?"

Rose climbed out of the comfort of her seat and went to get the book. After she had settled herself again, she removed Will's glasses and polished them on his pocket handkerchief before placing them on the bridge of his nose. "There. Now you're ready to begin."

She kissed his mouth, a little peck at first, and then something deeper and longer, before cuddling against him once more.

Will opened the book. "*Nana had something in her mouth which proved to be the boy's shadow.*" He read a whimsical scene between Mrs. Darling, a respectable matron, and the family dog, who acted as her children's nanny.

Rose giggled at the description, and as Will continued on, she kept smiling because her happiness was so complete.

That sign announcing *Rose Gardener's Florist* had once been the pinnacle of her pride and joy. Now she had added on something—someone—who made her life even richer and fuller. Surely no woman in the world could be as perfectly content as she.

CHAPTER TWENTY-ONE

"WE HAVE PUT in several good hours of work," Rose announced as she stepped away from the worktable to view the floral arrangements for the event.

"I will go to the venue and oversee they are delivered safely, giving you ladies sufficient time to dress and prepare," Will promised.

Rose went to wash her hands at the sink. Her sleeves rolled to the elbows made him want to stop her and pepper kisses over her pale forearms, but there was no time for any sidetracks on this important day.

"I am very excited. This is a once in a lifetime event. Hattie is quite nervous, this being her first time," Rose said. "I presume you'll meet Guy there."

Will nodded. "He's been awaiting this date with great anticipation. No doubt he's already pacing. I'll quickly wash up and change into the suit I've brought along, if that is all right."

"Certainly. You may use my room, then drive on ahead, but first..." She threw her still damp arms around his neck and met his mouth in a long, passionate kiss. "Surely a moment's delay won't make a difference," Rose whispered.

She clung to him as Will lifted her and seated her on the table amidst the detritus of stems and leaves. The fragrance of crushed blossoms rose around them as he kissed and touched her until his cock demanded he lay her back on the table and carry out its natural mandate.

Bad form. He would remain patient until the wedding night. That was what they had both decided, but it was becoming harder and harder to wait.

At length with his hair in wild swirls from Rose's fingers plunging through it, and his glasses knocked askew, one arm bent, Will dragged himself back from temptation.

"We'd better hurry. Wouldn't do to be late for this occasion," he reminded her softly.

"You're right. Of course, you are right, but oh, Will. I think we might have to set our wedding date soon, for I don't know how much longer I can bear this longing."

He preened at her confession. How could he not feel a little smug and manly at such words? Lifeblood, like a great engine, throbbed in him, and it wasn't only to do with passion or lust. There was so much occurring now in his formerly staid existence. A river of energy rushed through what had once been a desert.

Rose was the font from which it sprang.

She loves me, and one day soon I *will stand at an altar and watch her approach me up the aisle.*

THE VENUE WAS beautifully decorated with bunting enough to swaddle St. Paul's Cathedral, and Rose's enormous sprays of flowers brought life and color to the room. Every seat was filled, the rustle of clothing and the murmur of several hundred voices carrying on whispered conversations the only sounds in the hushed room.

Rose leaned toward Hattie, who was gazing wide-eyed at every detail. "Are you ready?"

"I believe so. I never thought I'd arrive at this point, but yes, I do believe I am ready for it."

"Good." Rose squeezed her hand. "I'll be right beside you, sisters-in-arms so to speak."

Hattie nodded.

An organist began to play, and the crowd rose as one to sing:

Rise up, women, for the fight is hard and long,
Rise in thousands singing loud a battle song.
Rise is might, and in its strength we shall be strong.
And the cause goes marching on.

When their anthem, sung to the tune of "John Brown's Body", was finished, Mrs. Pankhurst took the podium and began the rally. The Women's Parliament of 1907 had begun.

Rose looked at Will sitting on her other side, his expression intent as he listened to the rousing speech. She wondered what he felt. This was not truly his fight, even though he, like Guy, supported the cause. There were only a few men sitting amidst a crowd of hundreds of women. The men would show their solidarity here, but had been asked by the suffrage leaders not to participate in the march to Parliament.

Will must have felt her gaze for he looked at her and smiled. His breath brushed her temple when he leaned to whisper, "It is a brave thing you are about to attempt. Are you certain you won't allow me to walk with you in case things get out of hand? I want to be there to protect you and we both know how good I am with fisticuffs now."

She shook her head. "I love you for asking, but you know this is a walk we must take alone."

He did not insist or try to further convince her that he knew what was best. He did not act as if she did not understand the possible consequences of her actions. For those things, Rose loved him all the more.

Anticipation and dread vibrated through her as the stirring speech came to a climax. After attending meetings and planning bold moves, Rose was now about to take action. Her reputation, her body, perhaps even her life, might be at stake before they entered the great halls of Parliament to force the statesmen to hear their plea for the vote. A march of almost four hundred women would not be ignored by the police, who might arrest them at any point along the walk.

Rose noticed Guy holding Hattie's hand, offering his strength and solidarity. Hattie had contributed to the movement through only donations until now. Entering the front lines of the fight was a courageous move for the cautious woman. Meanwhile, Candace sat quietly on Rose's left, her gloved hands folded primly in her lap as if she attended a church service. The young woman had more grit than Rose had imagined upon their first meeting. She would not falter and since her guardian had legally released her, there was no one to stop her from having her say.

From the dais, a resolution was passed to condemn the omission of women's suffrage from the King's Speech, and a motion made to take the resolution to the Prime Minister.

Mrs. Pankhurst ended the rally with a cry, "Rise up, women!"

A roar of "Now!" and "Hear, hear!" shook Caxton Hall as the assembly rose as one.

As their row emptied to join the procession, Rose turned to Will. "I love you very much. I wish I could invite you to walk with me, but..."

"I understand. I will be there to bail you out of jail if the need arises." He hugged her so fiercely she could hardly breathe before letting her go. "It is a long walk from here to Westminster Abbey, and there may be stones thrown along the way. Protect yourself."

Rose nodded. Tears filled her eyes as she filed into the aisle and linked arms with Hattie and Candace.

The marchers emerged into bright sunshine, resuming the refrain, *Rise up, women, for the fight is hard and long*. Rose spotted one very tall man keeping pace with the march while weaving past the reporters and onlookers lining the route. From a distance, Will caught her eye and gave her a nod, encouraging her onward.

THE END

AUTHOR'S NOTE

The Women's Parliament actually took place on February 13, 1907 at Caxton Hall, concluding with a march to present their case to Parliament. I moved the date for dramatic purposes in my story.

From "Today in London suffrage history, 1907: the Women's Parliament ends in scuffles at Parliament" [Link]:
pasttenseblog.wordpress.com/2018/02/13/today-in-london-suffrage-history-1907-the-womens-parliament-ends-in-scuffles-at-parliament

> *"When the first contingents reached the green beside Westminster Abbey, the police announced that the procession could continue no further. The women refused to halt. As they went forward, mounted policemen began to ride through their ranks, in an attempt to break up the march, and constables on foot seized women and shoved them down side streets and alleys [sic]. The struggle continued for several hours, as bedraggled women hurled themselves again and again against the police. Fifteen women managed to reach the lobby, where they were promptly arrested."*

> By 10 p.m. the melee had ended. For the first time, arrests had not been confined to a handful of WSPU leaders – fifty-one women had been arrested in addition to Charlotte Despard, and Sylvia and Christabel Pankhurst.

About the Author

New York Times and *U.S.A. Today* Bestseller Bonnie Dee began inventing stories as a child, when she was the designated ghost tale teller at sleepovers. Writing childish stories on a yellow legal pad evolved into inventing fan fiction romances and later into writing for publication. Bonnie enjoys reading stories about people damaged by life who find healing with a like-minded soul. When she couldn't find enough books to suit her taste, she began to write them.

Taking the parasol approach to writing—a different color for every ensemble, she has dabbled in many romance sub-genres including historical, contemporary, paranormal, fantasy, and mystery. During years of collaboration with author Summer Devon, the pair produced many gay historicals, including a couple of Rainbow Award winners.

Now she is embarking on a new adventure set in her favorite Edwardian time period. "Modern inventions are making inroads into an old-fashioned society. The clash of the two is endlessly fascinating to me. Plus, I *love* the fashions! Looking at you Rose's beaded dress in Titanic."

bonniedee.com
facebook.com/bonnie.dee.144
facebook.com/BonnieDeeAuthor
Twitter: @bonnie_dee
bonniedeeauthor@gmail.com

Made in the USA
Monee, IL
20 February 2021

60217440R00098